More Praise for Such a Dangerous Silence and Harry Koumrouyan

In this saga, all the characters tinker as well as they can, oscillating between silence, oblivion, flight and denial.
— **La Tribune de Genève**

A text remarkable for its delicacy and its humanity.
— **Plume au Vent**

A universal story, shared by all pilgrims who have trodden the roads of exile.
— **France Arménie Magazine**

Groping in the dark, the novelist slowly unveils his story and covers it again, before revealing its multiple layers, the ebb and flow of a violent wave.
— **Djemâa Chraïti**

Also by Harry Koumrouyan

<u>Published by L'Aire (Switzerland)</u>
Un si dangereux silence, novel, 2016
L'Impératrice des Indes, novel, 2018
Courir dans les vagues, novel, 2021
Panne dans le métro, short story,
in Le monde est un village, 2017
La révolution d'octobre, short story,
in Naissances, 2018
Retour à l'union, short story,
in Pour Michel Moret, 2018

<u>Published by Auzou (France)</u>
L'enlèvement d'Elisa, novel, 2021

<u>Published by La 5ème saison (Switzerland)</u>
La maison où naquit, short story, 2018

<u>Published by Antipodes (Switzerland)</u>
Lettre à Antony Krafft-Bonnard, in Sauver les enfants,
sauver l'Arménie, 2020

SUCH A DANGEROUS SILENCE

A Novel

Harry Koumrouyan

Translated by
Kim Sanabria

CreateTankPress
New York

CreateTank
Bronx, New York, US.

CreateTank on the web and social media:
www.orlandoferrand.net/createtank
Facebook: www.facebook.com/mycreatetank/
Email: createtankmedia@gmail.com.

2022 CreateTank English First Edition. Translation from the French by Kim Sanabria.
Such a Dangerous Silence. Copyright © 2023 by Harry Koumrouyan.

2016 L'Aire (Switzerland) First French Edition.
Un si dangereux silence.

Acquisitions / Copy Editor / Robert F. Cohen.

Book design by Orlando Ferrand.

CreateTank books may be purchased for educational, business, or sales purposes. For information about exclusive discounts for bulk purchases, please email createtankmedia@gmail.com.

Library of Congress / US Programs, Law, and Literature Division Cataloging in Publication Program.

Manufactured and printed in the United States of America.

ISBN: 979-8-218-00047-9

Contents

Harry Koumrouyan

ACKNOWLEGMENTS

I am deeply thankful to Kim Sanabria, who translated this novel from the French. During the process, we kept in close contact, which allowed me to appreciate the extreme attention she gave to every detail of the original text. Kim is not only a translator in this endeavor, but also a bridge builder between two cultures that are simultaneously close together and far apart.

There were also two other key contributors, my dear friend Robert Cohen, who worked with Kim on the final draft of the translation, and Orlando Ferrand, who agreed to publish the text. Many, many thanks.

When writing this novel, I benefited from the generous help and encouragement of Courtney Elizabeth Mauk, Anne-Sophie Monglon, and Anne Noschis. Their suggestions were invaluable.

I would like to thank the friends that supported me on a trip that took me from Switzerland to Armenia via New York: Nancy Agabian, Chris Atamian, Viviane Fradkoff Sorokine, Gerald Herrmann, Olena Jennings, Christine Leimgruber, Irene and Sisvan Nigolian, and Jo Sarzotti.

My gratitude goes to my Swiss publisher, Michel Moret, whose door and phone lines were always open to me. Thank you, Michel, for believing in this story and giving it a chance. Your trust means more than I can say.

My son Adrien was my first reader and my assistant when my technical incompetence on the computer surfaced, which unfortunately happened at a frequent rate…

Finally, let me respectfully mention the numerous authors — historians, journalists, novelists —who, more and more often as time goes by, have rescued the Armenians and their history from the oblivion to which they have often been subjected.

Harry Koumrouyan

from the TRANSLATOR'S Journal

Entwined within our DNA, we carry markers connecting us to ancestors we have never met. Yet, as Harry Koumrouyan reminds us in this sweeping study of an Armenian family, we bear the imprint of more than just our genes. The present is a crescendo of history's accumulated days; the struggles of our ancestors also seep indelibly into our own existence. <u>Such a Dangerous Silence</u> is the kind of narrative that speaks to us all with its universal themes of ambition, regret, desire and loss. But perhaps more deeply, in its poignant exploration of the domino effect of our forebears' experiences, the novel speaks to a more profound sense of the past's acute significance for the present. Joseph Landolt is the young cellist whose emergence into manhood functions as a framework for the tale of his family. The story is set against the backdrop of the ruthless and systematic destruction of the Armenian people under Ottoman rule, which began in the last decade of the nineteenth century and persisted until the 1920s. Joseph's relatives have fled to Geneva, Switzerland, where he was born, and the exodus is latent in their every interaction. As the family grapples with the pervasive reverberations of the massacre of their compatriots and the near obliteration of their civilization, they try to disentangle themselves from a bygone era. They are resolved to succeed and take pride in their achievements, yet if they fail to speak about the forcible expulsion from their country, they tread a perilous path, one which Joseph will inevitably uncover.

Echoes of former times are difficult to communicate in a new vernacular. Aram, the family patriarch, finds this to be the case as he seeks to open his grandson's eyes to the torment of his family. Their yearnings, missteps, and fraught relationships are indeed a source of intrigue for Joseph, but the tragedy of a century ago seems so remote to this young musician with disheveled hair, more involved in his own intricate encounters with adolescence than with the fractured and sprawling lives of his relatives. I thought of Aram often as I translated the novel, of the hardships he must have faced, of his desire to release his grandson into a brighter future while at the same time educating him about the genocide that severed them so mercilessly from their roots. How could I do justice to such topics in yet another language, another era?

This novel, with its wide array of characters and their diverse experiences, was beautiful to translate. Its vocabulary is nuanced and distinctive. It has cinematic, gripping episodes, occasionally punctuated by dreams, visions, and literary references. The growing climax, centered on Joseph, is a *tour de force*, and I frequently found myself listening to the demanding pieces that he tackles on his cello as he attempts to come to terms with himself, soothe his emotions, please a stranger, or celebrate his grandfather's life. Yes, the translation was conceptually demanding, yet just as the novel is instructive, engrossing, and joyful, so was my task. Kudos to my cherished friend Harry Koumrouyan, a talented writer who rose to the challenge of encapsulating this critical history within a tale of triumph.

Kim Sanabria

SUCH A DANGEROUS SILENCE

Harry Koumrouyan

Prologue

My name is Joseph, and I want to leave Armenia. Armenia is not even where I live: instead, Armenia lives inside me. Its aroma fills me, intoxicates me, invades me.

My name is Joseph, and I'm eighteen years old. Last year, I lost my grandfather Aram, and with him, my roots, the cords that connected me to a mysterious, incomplete past.

My name is Joseph, and at night, I sometimes slowly whisper the syllables of that country I do not know: Armenia. Now, I want to turn the page on the tragedy that drove my ancestors from their land.

My name is Joseph, and this is the scandalous, unspeakable desire I am keeping to myself: I am leaving Armenia, where I have even never been. Maybe I want to abandon Armenia before it abandons me and forgets me forever.

Harry Koumrouyan

PART ONE

The Simonian Family

I

Letters from Inés Miranda

T he plane to Geneva hit an air pocket and pitched forward. "Passing through an area of turbulence," the captain announced. "Fasten your seatbelts and make sure your seats are in the upright position." The woman sitting next to Arthur Simonian appeared terrified. She pressed her hands together, then she drew them apart. First she rested her face against the window pane, then she leaned toward Arthur and muttered indistinctly. He was unwilling to enter into conversation and did not respond. Instead, he brandished the magazine in front of him like a protective screen and pretended to read. As it failed to discourage her, he muttered, "Sorry, I'm not feeling well." To his relief, the woman began to rummage in the seat pocket. She dug out some tiny earphones, then called the flight attendant over to help her select a music channel. Twenty minutes later, the plane resumed a calmer path, and the woman's anxiety seemed to retreat. Her features relaxed and she closed her eyes.

The flight attendants served an insipid meal, but Arthur did not touch it. He drank water instead of eating, hoping in vain to control the foreboding that had taken hold of him since takeoff. He had begun to correspond more frequently with his father, Aram Simonian, who had been sick for some months; perhaps he was attempting to recoup the long periods lost to silence or small talk. The messages sent between them had been short and factual at first, but had recently become more regular. Arthur lived in New York, where he taught French at a private school, while Aram became more fragile by the day. He would pass his days bent over his desk in Geneva, the city where his son had grown up but had left several years earlier.

5

Aram's health had deteriorated before Christmas, and Arthur cancelled a long-planned trip to the Caribbean. He decided to go back to a Europe that he did not quite recognize, as if he were listening to an old-fashioned tune and all that he remembered was the chorus. Little by little, he had broken away from his old habits, the people he knew, the places he liked frequenting, and the daily issues that used to form such a familiar, unchangeable routine. Fifteen years earlier, he had not intended to emigrate for good. However, at a certain point, he realized that a line, like a demarcation, now separated his past from his life in New York. There had been a split in his personality. He had passed through a mirror, crossed this dividing line, and become transformed in America. Now he lived in another language, operated within an alternate culture, and dressed in a different suit. He was no longer a hesitant young man, but an adult. Tonight, the plane was catapulting him back toward a bygone era, awakening images that had remained dormant within his memories until that moment.

These memories now rose to the surface, disorganized and nostalgic. Aram would come into his bedroom on Sunday mornings before breakfast and begin the ritual, always asking the same question. It never needed completing: "Arthur, would you like to…?" That was the signal the boy was hoping for. Aram was inviting Arthur to accompany him to the jewelry store he owned in the center of town. Lying impatiently in wait, the son was ready before he was even asked. He had already slipped on some pants and chosen a blue shirt, the one his father liked, which was on the small side already. In the street, the child forced himself to walk as quickly as Aram, lengthening his pace to keep up. In winter, Aram wore a beige cashmere coat and a hat (although hats had largely disappeared as fashionable accessories of the time). He was the most handsome father in the world, and the gratified boy glowed with pride. They had to go through a concealed door to get into the store, which was carefully barricaded with a metal bracing and a double access code. But when the gate was unlocked, Arthur found himself in Ali Baba's cave. It was a magical world for him, a world inhabited by princesses, counts, and queens from the Far East. The rings and watches sparkled, accentuated by the subdued light; the necklaces of precious stones, inaccessible inside their closed cabinet, seemed haughty, as if trying to scorn their visitors. Yet the magnificent scene belied its humble beginnings. Aram never spoke of his past, so Arthur had only learned the surprising and incomplete details of his parents' road to exile once he was an adolescent. It had been a long, rough, and violent journey.

Inside the jewelry shop, Aram sat in the little sales office, took out the documents with his name at the top, checked the accounts and prepared the week's orders. One day, Arthur had talked back to his father (or maybe fought with his sister). He was not allowed to go along with him ("You are going to have to stay home," Aram had declared.) He still remembered the disappointment.

Would Aram still be alive when the plane landed, this father who had always represented strength and safety for his children? Or would Arthur arrive too late? He knew that his sister Anne, whose actual name was Anoush, would be waiting for him at the airport. He imagined the silent look he was bound to see on her face. He could envisage her silhouette in the crowd, unconscious of the noise around her. He was certain that she would not move, waiting for him to go up to her first.

The plane's loudspeaker sputtered, and the captain announced the weather forecast. Some showers were expected for the rest of the day, and it might even snow. Looking out, Arthur could see a grey sky, forming its familiar winter canopy over the city. The plane touched down and the captain slammed on the brakes as they approached the gate. Customs formalities completed, Arthur located his luggage on the carousel and went through a glass partition. The panels opened with a metallic click as passengers approached. He saw Anne leaning against a pillar, and went up to her, but before she could utter even one word, he understood that he had arrived too late. She gave him a quick hug. "Arthur, you didn't get here in time." Her comment lingered in the air. "You didn't make it." This was obvious, so her reproach seemed unjust. He wanted to reply, but stopped because the airport was full of passengers arriving for the end-of-year celebrations, and it was not really the place for a family scene, one that would no doubt deteriorate. Explanations could wait until they were alone, as could the tangle of blame, misunderstandings, and recriminations – the "I told you so's." Anne added, "He died at six o'clock this morning." Though expected and dreaded, her announcement was so dry, so curt, that it stopped Arthur in his tracks. For a few moments, he could hardly absorb or understand his sister's words. "He died this morning…" he repeated under his breath, incredulous.

Anne lowered her head, but did not move. He would have liked to drop the stiff demeanor they were used to and take her into his arms, but how to shed the shyness and embarrassment inculcated in them during childhood? Anne pointed toward the exit. "Let's go. I'm parked close by." He followed her, navigating his suitcase around the waiting chauffeurs. They were waving signs with travelers' names scrawled in capital letters, and a sense of joy and excitement in the air. Passengers were greeted with hugs and exclamations, and a young man held up a rose encased in plastic. Arthur bumped awkwardly into a woman carrying a large bag, and was rewarded with a dirty look. "My father died this morning!" he wanted to shout. "Can't you understand?" Sitting in Anne's blue convertible, he kept repeating to himself insistently, "This is my city. This is my sister. My father just died." He held onto the words in order to fight a growing feeling of dizziness. He recognized the passenger from the airplane, who was hailing a taxi nearby. She smiled at him, no doubt relieved that the trip had ended with no problems. He nodded at her distractedly.

A silence descended on them in the car, despite all the things that they had to say. At this early hour, traffic was light. They crossed town quickly and went up the hill, where you could see the waters of Lake Geneva and, in the distance, the Jura Mountains. Anne slowed down as they got closer and, with the same precision that characterized all of her gestures, parked the car with a few deft movements of the steering wheel. Arthur heard the low notes of a cello as they went into the house. "Joseph is practicing his pieces. He has an exam soon," Anne said. Arthur hadn't seen his nephew for two years, but when Joseph appeared in the corridor, he recognized him immediately, even though the boy had grown. He was an adolescent now, still as thin as ever, with the same wild hair. Arthur kissed him on the cheek and, resting his hand on his shoulder, smiled. "Joseph, is that really you?" "I don't know…" his nephew replied. "Are you my uncle from New York?" He had always called him 'my uncle from New York,' and Arthur liked the nickname. Some years before, Joseph and his mother had gone over to visit him. Arthur remembered his terrified expression in a Broadway theater when they went to a performance of *The Phantom of the Opera*, which included a stream of special effects. He could still hear his nephew's exclamation as they looked at the lights in the city, gazing over its twinkling expanse from the terrace of the Empire State Building: "Fantastic!" They had scoured the biggest store in the world to find the red basketball sneakers that Joseph absolutely had to have. They had spent a week of laughter and discovery, interspersed with visits to the muffled halls of museums, spicy food in Mexican restaurants, and the colors of the maple trees in the parks. And yet, Anne never followed up on Arthur's repeated invitations to go back to New York with her son. "Not now; next year, perhaps…" she would say.

Glancing inquisitively in his uncle's direction, Joseph asked,

"So, you heard about Granddad?"

"Yes, but I can hardly believe it. It happened so suddenly…"

"It didn't happen suddenly," Anne corrected him as they went into the living room. "The hospital had put us on the alert."

"I misunderstood the warnings, obviously… I was under the impression that you were blowing things out of proportion."

"No, it seems to me that you just didn't want to know. You had your head in the clouds."

"Perhaps. For me, *hayrig*[1] has always been the same strong man I knew as a child."

"You wouldn't say that if you had seen him. He was getting weaker and weaker by the day. You should have come back earlier…"

Her jaw clenched, Anne sat upright in a beige armchair near the window, adopting the impeccable posture of the older sister who knows everything. Teaching her brother a lesson had always been one of her favorite activities, and at that moment Arthur resented her, even though in the past they had been 'accomplices,' as their parents called them, because they were so closely connected. But he did feel the

---

[1] Father

need to recognize the responsibilities that Anne had undertaken."It's true, you were really busy with our parents, and you shouldered all the responsibility, especially after *mayrig*'s[2] death. Let's be honest…"

"That's a shallow comment, don't you think?"

Anne got up and opened the window. A fresh breeze came in, lifting the net curtains. Seagulls shrieked, circling the grey lake. Inside the immaculate room, every piece of furniture, every ornament (a collection of frosted glass animals, some dolls brought back from a trip to Africa…) had been meticulously arranged, as if the room were soon to be photographed for a decorating magazine. Arthur felt as if he were in a foreign land.

In a 'sweet and sour' tone of voice, Anne said,

"Come on now, king Arthur, you have a beautiful life. No children. Kind, beautiful lady friends. Trips…"

"We could change the subject if you like. Let's talk about Eric instead. How is he?"

Anne's tumultuous relationship with her husband, Eric Landolt, was littered with separations and reconciliations, and she did not reply.

"So you're not saying anything?" Arthur insisted.

"I don't want to talk about Eric. He isn't here today. He'll be back tomorrow. Maybe."

Joseph stepped in, since this was obviously the beginning of a fight.

"I'm making coffee. Anyone want some?"

Anne and Arthur accepted at the same time, which managed to divert the discussion. When they'd finished their coffee, Joseph picked up the bow to his cello.

"I'm going to play *The Swan* by Saint-Saëns. Grandpa always liked this piece."

---

[2] Mother

The boy sat calmly with his instrument close to his body. The wood of the cello gave off a warm sound. When he finished playing the piece, with a breadth and gravity surprising for his age, Joseph didn't move for a moment. Then he smiled. There was silence.

Aram had been sick for some time. A general weakness had taken possession of his body, but not his spirit. So, when he asked his daughter to visit him more frequently, first at his house and later at the clinic, it was with a kind of shyness that was not customary for him. Anne liked seeing him, talking to him, touching him. She had asked the doctors and understood: he would not live for very much longer. There was no exit on the road ahead. She had always been close to her father, and even though his imminent death saddened her, Aram's serenity softened her grief. One evening, when she was sitting by his side at the hospital, he pushed his meal aside and said, "You know, I've been very lucky. I can't complain." When she left the room, Anne saw a nurse in the corridor. She appeared to be waiting for her.

"Your brother lives in New York, right? It might be time for him to…"

Her idea was not fully articulated, but Anne finished the sentence for her.

"…for him to come back. You're right. I'll alert him this evening."

The typical line ("The prognosis is poor") had not been spoken aloud, but there was no longer any doubt about the outcome.

For a few hours, Anne couldn't decide what to do. Finally, she called her brother, but got the distinct impression that he refused to believe her. It was as though

Arthur wanted to convince both himself and his sister that their father was fine. He stated forcefully,

"You're getting yourself all worked up about nothing. The man is rock solid. He's going to carry on, I'm sure."

"Not this time, I'm telling you."

"How do you know? Did you see the doctor?"

She forced herself to remain calm.

"I spoke to the nurse. She was the one who advised me to warn you. It's serious, and there's no point denying it."

Arthur didn't respond right away, but then he disclosed that he was planning a trip to the Caribbean during the Christmas vacation. "That's the issue, and he's finally admitting it," Anne thought.

"Well, as you wish … but I think that you should put off your vacation until later. The Caribbean can wait."

"Yes, I know, but I'm not going alone."

She understood, of course, but she was not concerned about the details. She thought, "He has a new girlfriend, the flirt. That's where his priorities lie. Putting obligation before pleasure has never been Arthur's strong suit." But since her brother was almost forty-two years old now, she was tired of repeating that he had to put his family first from time to time. He needed to take some responsibility.

"OK," he said, finally taking her at her word. "I'll find a flight and get there as soon as I can. Will you come and pick me up at the airport?"

Their parents had assigned contrasting characteristics to their children. Arthur embodied lightness, charm, and ease whereas his older sister was an exemplary student, the best in the class. She was the favorite of the piano teacher, who drew stars all over her sheet music. In fact, Ms. Clerc considered Anne exceptionally gifted, and always gave her a packet of soft candy to show her satisfaction. When Arthur knew that his sister was coming home, he would wait greedily for her, asking a mischievous question that was more like a statement. "You're going to give me some. Right?"

One afternoon, the children were alone in the living room after school. Arthur was jumping on the white leather sofa and almost fell off. To regain his balance, he reached out his left hand, and knocked over a Chinese vase. A second later, the vase was in pieces on the floor. With a disconcerting ease, Arthur transformed himself into a mere witness. He threw his sister a look of surprise (as if to say, "What just happened?") and went into his bedroom, leaving the fragments of porcelain, adorned with colorful dragons, scattered over the floor. When *hayrig* and *mayrig* came back home that evening and found the broken vase, they interrogated the children one by one. The boy was determined not to get punished, and tried to hide the fact that he was the culprit. His calm assurance did not let him down, and Anne took the rap in his place. "Your brother is younger than you. If we are not there, it's your job to watch over him. You're a big girl now." There were only two years between them, so Anne was consumed by a feeling of injustice that would linger long after the incident had passed. She was resentful of Arthur for having kept such a straight face, such a perfect sense of calm when faced with their parents' questions. (At the airport, as she was waiting for her brother, Anne was convinced that he would appear with the same straight face and settled features, the same perfect sense of calm, as if he were getting ready to take part in an elegant Christmas Eve celebration. Far from her, impossible to reach.)

Anne had wanted to be closer to her brother when she was an adolescent, and to discover the world he was growing up in. It was in vain, because he kept both his secrets and his friends to himself. (She recognized, nonetheless, that she did the same.) She had a secret crush on one of Arthur's friends, a boy with black hair and a coy smile. She always wanted to talk to him when she saw him, but it was impossible. Lucien had hardly rung the door to the apartment when Arthur would rush to welcome him and drag him into his room. A moment later, sitting at her desk, and leaning distractedly over some Latin homework, she would hear an English singer with a husky voice that made the walls shake. Lucien occasionally shared meals with the Simonian family. Anne would try to engage him in conversation, but the boys quickly shifted topics, which shut her out. They wanted to discuss ice hockey and the latest successes of their favorite team. A long time later, when she learned that Lucien had gotten married, she experienced a pang of disappointment, something like melancholy, as if an opportunity had passed her by. Nothing allowed her to actually think so, but she had a very lively imagination.

Fifteen years had now passed since Arthur left Europe for New York, and Anne missed him a lot. A strong camaraderie had linked them since they were children, yet their close bond did not preclude disagreements or misunderstandings. When Anne took her son to visit her brother, she was in the throes of a marital conflict. She wanted Arthur to listen closely to her story and to give her support. She forced herself not to cry, and reined in her emotions in accordance with the customs of their upbringing: "Stand up straight and hold back your tears." Arthur paid close attention, but then he put his hand on her arm and said, "Anne, you are going to get through this. You love your husband, no matter what. Don't become bitter…" He did not understand, or would not admit, that she needed this bitterness, and even found pleasure in it. But in spite of this, the stay in New York went well, especially for Joseph. Arthur assumed the privileged role that the maternal uncle plays in some societies, and did his utmost to please his nephew. The highlight of the vacation was a pair of basketball sneakers with an LED light in the heels. Joseph was thrilled with the shoes, and he wore them until they got a hole in the sole, and the small colored bulbs stopped flashing.

The day before, at two o'clock in the morning, Anne got the call that she both expected and feared. She recognized the nurse's voice, slightly out of breath: "Mrs. Landolt, your father's condition has deteriorated. I think you should come now…" Anne could not decide whether to wake Joseph, and decided to go to the hospital alone. When she got to Aram's bedside, he was breathing in fits and starts, indifferent to the knot of tubes delivering oxygen to him. She sat at the very edge of the bed and took his hand. He opened his eyes and tried to speak. Little by little, his breathing slowed down. The dawn gently arrived. A pale December light lit up the room. Aram died. She watched him attentively. The illness had left its trace on his face, but he was still handsome, as he had always been. "Now I am an orphan," she thought. "Even an adult can be an orphan. I've lost my father. I have lost my Armenia." She remained motionless in the room. A few moments later, the door opened and the nurse entered. She looked hard at Aram and understood that he was gone, but to Anne's relief, she did not immediately commence with the professional procedures that she was supposed to carry out. Anne felt a strange intimacy with this unknown woman, one for whom Aram would now become a mere body that she must attend to with an established protocol within a fixed timeframe. A curtain of solitude fell over Anne, who lowered her head. "Come on, I'll make you a cup of coffee," the nurse said.

When Anne left the hospital, a throng of activity had replaced the calm of the night before. Once on the street, she was so disoriented that she couldn't remember where her car was. She sat on a bench and called Joseph to tell him that his grandfather had passed away. "And I can't find the car," she added.

Joseph could not stop himself from laughing. "Mom, you're incredible. Take a careful look around…"

The tone of his voice consoled her. She felt a little better. She looked up, and saw that the car was parked right in front of her.

"Oh, wait… There, I've found it. It's already time for me to go to the airport. I'll go and get Arthur, and we'll be right back."

After Joseph hung up, he got out a blue notebook, buried at the bottom of a drawer. He sometimes kept a journal.

Granddad died this morning. My poor grandfather! I'm going to miss him a lot, I already know it. I loved spending time with him, especially when we were alone. ("When we were alone": Joseph didn't want to write that phrase in the past. It sounded wrong. At school, the teacher would note in the margin: "Verb tense error. Correct it.") The boy continued: *Aram, my grandfather, would often take me down to the lake. We walked on the jetty, and then we would stop and he would buy me an ice cream. It always ran down my fingers. And he told me about the jewelry store. At first, it was a small shop with very few customers, and he had a hard time. Then success came, "through sheer hard work," as he put it. That was one of his favorite expressions. He would also say, "At first, we had nothing. Not a penny. We had to fight for everything."*

Before he came to Geneva, he lived with his brother and sister Becca in the Ottoman Empire. Then they were banished, and they came here. I don't understand their story very well, and when I asked questions, he never actually replied. He said: "Pasha, I'll tell you about that later." Now, it is too late. Well, it's better this way. You don't live in the past: you live in the present. I liked it when he said "pasha" with his Armenian accent. After so many years, Granddad had kept his accent. I had gotten so used to it that I barely heard it any more. Except on the phone. I wonder why… Perhaps the sound is amplified!

When Mom came out of the hospital after her father died, she couldn't find her car. She is upset, it's normal, but I know her: she is going to hold back her grief, just like she always does. She acts controlled and self-assured, instead of letting herself go. And yet, you have to mourn your loved ones: you're not going to drown in your sorrow!

I'm happy to see Arthur again. I love him, my Uncle Arthur. And one day, I would like to go back and visit him in New York.

Aram was buried before Christmas. In church, Joseph sat in the first pew beside his mother and uncle, who painted a picture of unity and affection. The boy knew that there was still some tension between them, and he admired the effort they made to hide it so skillfully. He couldn't refrain from thinking, "What good actors they are…" but he stopped himself from taking jabs at them, contenting himself with a discreet smile of complicity with his father, who sat in a row further back. Anne and Arthur were dressed elegantly. Anne had asked Joseph to put on a suit and tie, but he had refused. Jeans and a white shirt would be enough. "You could also do your hair nicely!" Joseph was sorry, but he did not do his hair nicely. Ever. And his hair was everything to him. He answered, "Granddad would not say anything, I'm sure." Despite her disappointment, Anne did not put up a fight. She felt vulnerable and was not going to get into an argument with her son over something so trivial.

The priest gave a lively but lengthy sermon on life after death. Once it was over, he moistened his lips with his tongue, and then turned toward Joseph, who got up, picked up his cello and sat facing the congregation. A chair had been placed beside the flower-covered coffin. Before playing *The Swan*, the boy spoke a few sober words: "I miss my grandfather, and I'm going to play a piece that he loved."

Joseph had never known such an attentive public. It was a shame that this was a funeral! Once the last note of *The Swan* had faded, he put down his bow. A deep silence enveloped the entire church, and then a solemn and beautiful Armenian song was played. The priest gave the blessing and the bells began to ring, quietly at first, but then louder and louder. Row after row, the congregation passed by Anne and Arthur, bowed and went outside.

In the crowd on the forecourt, there was a woman of about sixty years old, dressed in a black coat with a fur collar. She came up to the family. Anne and Arthur did not recognize her, but Joseph had met her at his grandfather's house. She stretched out a gloved hand and said in a low voice, "Hello, my name is Inés Miranda; I live in Guatemala. We've never met, but I was very close to Aram. I am so sorry that he has left us." And she added, pointing toward Joseph, "This young man is an excellent cellist. It was no surprise for me because I had already heard him play, and I am one of his admirers. When he gives his first performances in big concert halls across the world, I will be there. You can count on me." As she said these words in her beautiful Spanish accent, Inés Miranda stood on tiptoes. It was as if she were trying to sound more convincing by raising herself up a few centimeters. Anne was completely taken aback by this declaration, but remained impassive. There would be time, later, to question her son about this unknown woman. Joseph invited her to join them at a reception next to the church, and Inés accepted. "Thank you. I will toast to Aram's memory." They could make out the low purr of an engine. The black hearse, carrying the coffin and the flowers, was leaving. "It's over. He's leaving," Joseph thought. A tear rolled down his cheek.

In the evening, when everyone, even the distant cousins, had left with the usual promises ("We'll see you soon" and "I'll call you in a day or two"), Joseph heard his mother say to Arthur, "Before you go back to New York, we should go to *hayrig's* house together." She used the Armenian word to speak of their father.

Arthur moved his lips imperceptibly and Joseph, observing him, guessed that his uncle did not want to comply.

"Do you want to take an inventory?"

"I don't want to clear the house on my own. You have to help me."

"We can find someone to take care of it," Arthur proposed, trying to adopt a soothing tone.

"And then what? Call a second-hand dealer? Some guy comes over in his truck, loads up the furniture, and you find it at a flea market a week later? You're joking, I hope."

Joseph stared at them, both so tense with grief, separated by an apparently impassable distance, although he knew they had been so close before.

Arthur realized that he needed to give in. He said, simply,

"Let's go. Where's your car?"

This time, Anne knew where she had left the blue convertible. Joseph decided to go with them, thinking it better not to leave them alone. They crossed the countryside and drove along the lake. It was lined with tall trees, like lampposts rising out of the darkness. No one spoke as they went along, and the boy cast his mind back to the coffin, to Inés Miranda's coat, and the hearse that carried Aram away. He heard the loud voice of the priest, mixed in with the melody of the Armenian chant rising up to the church vaults.

They arrived. Aram's house, where he had lived since his wife's death, was partly hidden by hedges interspersed with red shrubs. The back of the building was flanked by a small tower with a round window, and from this observatory, you could follow the flight of birds which would migrate toward African shores before autumn began.

Anne searched for the keys in her bag, taking a moment to find them while Arthur undid the dark scarf tied under his coat. The clumsiness of their gestures did not escape Joseph. They looked as though they were filming a scene in slow motion. As they hesitated, the boy pushed the door open, no doubt wanting to encourage them to step inside. Passing through a narrow hallway, they went into the living room. The room had not been touched since Aram was urgently whisked away to the hospital. There was a paper spread out on the sofa, like a witness to its interrupted reading. By the side of a leather chair, on a small table, there was a half cup of coffee, and a fly had fallen into it. A library took up a whole section of the room, and books were stacked haphazardly when there was no room for them. On the opposite wall, a bright wall light illuminated a large abstract painting, bordered by a white frame. Each object seemed to announce the imminent return of the proprietor: you would have thought that he had left hastily, with the firm intention of coming back right away. The deceased was absent, yet he was more present than ever. He was no longer there, but his daily objects – his books, his table, his paintings – waited for him from their silent look-out posts. Only the fly, its wings folded in the liquid, had stopped living.

Arthur turned to his sister. "And now, what should we

do? I have to go back home soon." Anne had hung up her coat and was standing near the French windows opening onto the garden. "He is ready to make his escape back to New York as soon as possible," she thought. She said, "We can't empty this house. Or sell it. Not for the time being. We'll have to wait…"

"And leave things like this? I don't think so. It will be even more difficult three months from now."

Arthur walked over to the book shelves.

"No, don't do that!"

"I didn't touch anything."

"You were going to take down the books. I saw you."

"Anne, calm down. I didn't touch anything."

Neither of them said a word. They were two hostile strangers, frozen in a block of ice. Perhaps they expected to see Aram suddenly materialize in the room. He would have made some consoling remarks and given them the gentle words they needed. Joseph spoke up:

"You should wake up! You're like two people lost in a museum. Granddad would not want to see two ghosts in his house…"

"We're lucky you're here," Arthur remarked, derisively.

A mysterious noise pierced the silence. It was an owl, hooting in the night.

"Didn't you hear the warning?"

Neither Arthur nor Anne replied to the question. "Come," the boy said, pointing toward the landing. They climbed the narrow staircase inside the tower. Joseph opened the window, and, a moment later, they heard the owl again. Beside the window, on a low table with a glass top, they found a bundle of letters. They went over to the table. Arthur picked up the packet and muttered, "I've never seen that handwriting." He asked his sister if she had any idea who they were from, but she shook her head. Joseph came to their aid.

"At the funeral, that woman wearing a black coat with a fur collar. Remember?"

"Yes," said Anne." She came from Guatemala. I forget her name. Inés…"

"Inés Miranda."

"And so?"

Joseph smiled at them, hesitated a moment and then said, "You would never have suspected it, but grandfather and Inés were…very close."

"And we didn't know anything!" Arthur exclaimed.

Aram's children were unaware of their father's inner sanctum and the young cellist was proud of having been his grandfather's confidant. He had been granted the privilege of access.

"How did he meet that lady?" asked Arthur, who sometimes adopted his sister's dry intonation without realizing it.

"Remember… a few years ago, Aram took a long trip."

"Aram? Now you're calling him by his first name?"

"Yeah, so what? I used to call him by his first name sometimes, and he didn't mind a bit. Let me go back to the story. Listen up, because it's worth it."

Joseph reminded them of the guided tour in Central America that Aram took after his wife died. "I can't bear the grief here. I have to go somewhere else," he'd said. In Guatemala City, he left the other travelers in the humid heat of a summer evening and wandered aimlessly until he heard the sound of jazz. The melody came from a bar called Oh Là Là, with doors that opened onto the street. Aram went in, sat on a high stool and ordered a drink. From the neighboring table, a woman glanced over at him, and smiled. It was Inés, sipping on something sweet. They started to talk. She asked him where he was from, and other questions followed. The conversation flowed gently, and a bond started to form between them.

"… and then, oh là là! Joseph concluded. It's as simple as that."

"I just can't imagine my father meeting a woman that way," said Anne, looking at her brother. "What do you think?"

"Well, I think I've found the title of the book I want to write: *The Secret Life of Our Parents*," Arthur answered. "So, what happened next?"

"They saw each other the following day. Granddad pretended that he was sick, and missed the tour he was supposed to take. He preferred Inés to the Mayan ruins. You can't blame him!"

Anne knit her brow. Arthur, caught between surprise and sarcasm, began to smile. The boy continued, "Then, they met several times here in Geneva, and in Madrid, where Inés's son works as an architect."

"I wonder why he never said anything to us. And all this time, you knew what was going on."

"It's so easy to understand. Aram had become a young man again, and was having an affair. He was looking for some fun…"

"Excuse me? Please, Joseph."

"He wanted to have a good time, that's all. He said, 'Better to have a love affair than to write your will or visit the cemetery!'"

Anne and Arthur believed they knew everything about their father, and it took them a long time to admit that their image was so incomplete. To convince them, Joseph carefully took a photo out of his wallet, slipped inside several months earlier. The photo had been taken on a rowboat, and it showed Aram in a short-sleeved shirt holding the oars, while Inés stood beside him, her hand on his shoulder.

"It's so easy to understand," Joseph repeated.

For the first time since Arthur had returned from New

York, the atmosphere lightened up. On the glass table sat the pile of letters that Inés Miranda had written. A swan was stamped on the envelopes, its wings open as if ready to fly away.

"Well, Joseph, my boy, it looks like you've won this round," said Arthur. "Now, it's our turn. We're going to tell you some family stories that you don't know."

They went down to the living room. Anne made some tea, and they carried on talking until daybreak.

Later, Joseph wrote:

Not sure that I really want to hear all their stories. At the same time, I'm curious. To know where we come from. What we're made of. Things that happened before I was born, and that they never told me. People don't talk too much in this family, especially about painful memories. Now, it's as if the death of the patriarch has opened a dam. The floodwaters have been released, and we're all going to get swept away.

And Inés Miranda's correspondence? What are his heirs going to do with all those letters? Read them, throw them out, keep them? Oh là là...

Harry Koumrouyan

II

The Marriage Announcement

Nineteen years earlier. Sunday, April 24th. Late morning.

"I haven't seen *hayrig*. Is he around?" Arthur asked Anoush.

"He left at eleven. He went to get those orchids he ordered."

"Don't tell me he's starting with the orchids again. It's a total obsession! He'll be spending a fortune."

"Yes, but flowers mark important moments for him. Remember Christmas?"

"How could I forget? The whole living room was transformed into an exotic greenhouse."

"Yeah, and we could hardly breathe."

"He got pretty angry when we aired out the room and told him why."

Anoush selected some silverware from a careful display in a mahogany box, and imitated the husky accent that Aram Simonian retained, even after so many years in Geneva. "Good Lord, shut the window. The orchids will get cold. They're fragile, you know. Now that you don't live with your parents any more, you seem to prefer dreary apartments. Beautiful décor does nothing for you. It's such a pity. You should be happy that we're able to buy these beautiful flowers, even if they are expensive."

They joked around as they set the table, about the orchids' quirky shapes, their velvet petals, and their curved stems. The elevator made a noise. The patriarch was returning. They stopped talking in order to prevent an argument that would inevitably turn sour. The door opened

27

and in came Aram, carrying the orchids with great care. That day, the flowers had a different purpose than mere decoration: they represented an enduring tradition. The delicate question was the money they had cost. The money was not just a symbol of wealth, but evident proof that they had completely integrated into a new country. As Anoush put it succinctly, their parents had succeeded. They had overcome all the obstacles before them, going from poverty to material comfort. They had held tight to the prow of their boat, no matter what the obstacles thrown in their way by waves or winds. They seemed not to recognize fear or doubt, and even if they did, they never showed it. In a word, they were admirable, and their children did admire them, even if it was not that simple to have such admirable parents. Anoush and Arthur were not front-line soldiers. They had won the war without doing battle.

The dining room was ready for the family meal. "Don't forget the candlesticks," Victoria reminded her children. "I polished them this morning." She had taken out the linen tablecloth with lightly raised woven pomegranates. On the dresser, behind the formal table, *mayrig* placed the large wine bottles that Aram had taken out of the cellar the evening before. The meal took place in an elegant yet modest dining room. Aram and Victoria were prone to crossing the line of good taste without always realizing it. They were so intent on proving to the world that they were able to afford stylish furniture, antique mirrors and shimmering fabrics. Hence their unrestrained affection for the curtains in the hallway, too pink and too heavy. Despite their children's frequent objections, the parents would never get rid of them, and in fact, valued them above everything else.

Every year, on April 24th, the Simonian family would get together in commemoration of the Armenian genocide perpetuated by the Ottoman Empire a century earlier. Strangely, or perhaps not so strangely, each one fought against the sadness of the memory; they savored the generous portions of food that their mother and Aunt Becca had been preparing since dawn. There were stuffed vegetables, chicken with nuts, and salad with dried fruit and eggplants. They ate slowly. As tradition dictated, there were interruptions for a toast at regular intervals. Sitting at the head of the table, Aram gazed happily upon his family, everyone gathered together on such a solemn occasion. As he made the first toast, he grasped a small cross mounted on a stone pedestal, and raised it to the memory of those who had died during the massacres. He drank to the deceased and recited an Armenian prayer whose monotonous chant was familiar to Anoush and Arthur, even though they did not understand it. Their parents were to blame for that because they had never taught their children the language, fearing that it would turn them into strangers in the city where they were born. A stupid decision, Anoush and Arthur considered, undoubtedly the high price of an unconditional assimilation, and marked by a Francophilia that had become an obsession for Aram. He repeated to his children, as if he were speaking of a treasure all the more precious because it seemed inaccessible. "You have to know the language here to perfection. That is your key, your entrance ticket. It's the only way. The real way. It is more important than money." He had also illustrated his conviction by buying his family the great works of French literature, published in an expensive collection. From that point on, the books sat patiently on the living room bookcase, protected by real leather covers. Arthur and Anoush could clearly have made the effort to learn Armenian, drawing the beautiful letters of its alphabet and reciting the declinations of its verbs, but they never ventured down that path. They were comfortably settled in their lives in Geneva, far from roots that were now effaced and almost invisible, just like the Ottoman Empire itself.

When he heard the beginning of this story, Joseph wrote:

Of course I know that April 24ᵗʰ is an important date, but the tradition of the orchids and the family meals has been lost, probably for a long time now. We hold onto this past that now seems like a flimsy drawing in the sand. If a strong wave breaks over it, it will disappear. I would like to know our history better, but I feel as if I'm running after scraps, pieces of a puzzle that are impossible to put together. Only two or three objects represent our legacy. We kept the linen tablecloth with the red pomegranates, but we almost never use it. Mom says that it's difficult to iron, but I'm wondering if that is just an excuse. Sometimes, we prefer to tuck our happy memories away, like photos that we never look at because they make us feel nostalgic.

The commemorative meal was about to end when Anoush turned to each guest, gently raised her hand, and said: "Now I would like to make a toast." Becca, who was her godmother, watched her adoringly, granting her request. Anoush got up and remained silent for a moment, her lips trembling. Everyone wondered what she was going to say. To encourage her, Arthur poured her some champagne. But he was too awkward. The glass overflowed and bubbles spattered onto the tablecloth. "Don't worry," Becca reassured him. "Champagne doesn't leave any stains!" Anoush was slightly out of breath, as if she had been running. "Listen, please. I have an important announcement," she said. Then she stopped talking, which made them even more curious. They put down their cutlery, waiting for her to continue. Aram's eyes grew misty: Anoush, so intelligent and beautiful, was his jewel. She was going to breeze through her medical studies. Even though she had not passed her final exams yet, her father would announce, "My daughter is a doctor." (Arthur sometimes thought that this term, one he used with such pleasure, was the immigrant's sweetest revenge.) Anoush was not only an outstanding student, but an accomplished musician. When she played a Chopin waltz, her hands slid assuredly across the keys, nobody noticing any missed notes. Her father would sit blissfully on the right, eyes half closed, sunk in his favorite chair. She had hardly finished the piece when he clamored, "Play it for me one more time."

Aram loved his two children, but he secretly favored his daughter. If this feeling had ever risen to consciousness, he would be too uncomfortable to admit it. For a long time, Arthur had believed that his blue eyes, a rare characteristic among Armenians, had created a distance between him and his father. A son with eyes of such an unusual color! Aram had always criticized his character as being "a little too fickle," more inclined to playing than studying. In the evening, when he came home from the jewelry store, he hoped to find Arthur reading Balzac or trying to solve some complex equation. Instead, Arthur would be stretched out on his bed, exchanging jokes on the phone with his friend Igor. "Instead of making progress, this boy is wasting time," Aram thought bitterly. He wanted his son to be a brilliant scholar. Although he never stated it explicitly, he was sure that academic prowess would lead to exceptional success. Meanwhile, Anoush was hunched over her small desk, writing poetry for a competition run by a local newspaper. (She did not win the prize, but in the eyes of her family, she gained a reputation for talent and conscientiousness.)

Around the table, nobody spoke. Intrigued by the promise of her announcement, Arthur looked at his sister and loudly inquired: "So?" Anoush, overcoming her hesitation, rested her hands on the tablecloth and sighed, "I'm getting married."

There was such astonishment, that nobody asked any questions. Aram went pale, Becca laughed nervously, and Arthur was surprised. For once, his sister had not confided in him. Until then, Anoush had had "very close friends," as her mother put it obliquely, but never a serious boyfriend. Nice boys would come and go, and to Aram's relief, never reappear. Her most serious lover was an Italian computer technician called Lorenzo. When he went back home to Rome after a few months, Aram had discreetly removed his photo, which, alongside *Madame Bovary*, had taken center stage in the library.

"It can't be true, said *hayrig*, trying to overcome his surprise. You've never told us anything and all of a sudden, you're getting married… I don't believe you."

Aram's Armenian accent became stronger with emotion.

"But nevertheless, it's true, I promise you."

Decisive and leaving no room for compromise, Aram stated, "You're too young."

"You're forgetting that I'll be twenty-six next year. I don't need your permission to go down to the town hall. Look, many of my friends are already married."

"Of course, but they've finished studying and they even have jobs. They are already settled, which isn't the case with you." (Suddenly, her father remembered that she was not yet a doctor.)

"Don't get upset, *hayrig*. I'm not going to ask you for anything. I can take care of things on my own," said Anoush, trying to sound reassuring.

"That's not the issue."

"But who is this boy?" Victoria asked, forcing herself to speak calmly. "Your father is right. You've never told us about this relationship, and suddenly, just like that, from one day to the next…"

Her words drifted off. Anoush began again.

"Sometimes, you meet someone and you know that he's a good person. It's pointless waiting around!"

"Ah, I see," said her father dryly. "It was love at first sight."

"Honey," Becca began, in the voice she'd used in her acting career. "First of all, is he a good-looking young man? Do you have a photo?"

"Becca, this is not the time," Aram interrupted. "We'll see the photos later. I'd like to know if your… fiancé …" (he hesitated to say the word) "has a job."

"No, he's studying medicine with me. He's starting his internship next year."

"And his parents? Have you met them?" Victoria asked.

"No, I don't know them. They don't live here."

"But what will they think about their son getting married, if he hasn't even finished his degree yet?"

After a moment's hesitation, Anoush replied tersely, "They don't know anything about it."

"And why didn't he tell them? Isn't that a bit strange?

"They definitely wouldn't approve if they knew about it."

Aram felt a rush of paternal pride, which translated into a groan. A girl as beautiful and intelligent as Anoush should obviously have the whole world's approval.

"I'm very anxious to meet this boy," said Becca, delicately wiping her lips with the embroidered napkin and sitting upright in her chair, as if the fiancé were going to come in any minute. "Oh, and by the way, what is his name?"

Anoush did not reply. She seemed embarrassed: she looked at her brother, who sensed that a problem was on the horizon even though he could not identify it.

"She's marrying Mr. Anonymous," said Aram, sarcastically.

"He's not Mr. Anonymous. His name is Mehmet."

You could have cut the air with a knife when his name was pronounced.

"Mehmet?" *hayrig* asked. He acted as though he had misheard.

"Yes, Mehmet," Anoush repeated defiantly. "He's from Turkey."

Suddenly, the dining room seemed to collapse under the tension. Everyone held their breath. Aram hit the table with the flat of his hand, and started up, overturning the chair. His anger and surprise made him shudder. First, he headed toward the door. Then, hands twitching, he made a fist and waved it in the air. After that, he reconsidered and turned back again. Heavy and threatening, he walked over to his daughter, who hung her head. She looked scared that he would hit her. Her father had never raised a hand toward his children, but at that moment, he was so overcome with sadness that he had become a stranger to her. Aram managed to control his emotions. He leant over, gruffly picked up his chair, and put it back in place. He didn't speak for a few seconds, while his stunned family looked on at him. Then he wailed breathlessly, like a wounded animal.

"Now I understand why you didn't introduce us to this hustler. I want you to remember what day we are celebrating. It's the 24th of April."

As if trying to hammer his point home, he repeated, "April 24th."

"I know the date. I haven't forgotten it."

"So you did it on purpose?"

"Yes, in a sense, I did choose this moment to talk to you."

"You've lost your head, my poor girl," said Victoria, holding Aram's arm. "I would never have believed that you could be so insensitive."

Becca began to cry.

"Anoush should explain why she chose this date."

Arthur would have liked to speak up, but he was having trouble putting his ideas together. He had mixed feelings. His loyalty to his sister had always been strong, yet at the same time, he understood his parents' reaction, especially on this particular day. And, above all, he was hurt that Anoush hadn't confided in him.He interpreted her silence as betrayal.

"Don't you realize that these people have never recognized their crimes?" Aram asked, furiously pointing his finger at his daughter. "For us, Turkey is a forbidden country."

"Yes, I do realize that," Anoush answered, calmly. "But I would like to explain to you that Mehmet is now a part of my life, and I love him. Perhaps it is time to move on…"

"And then to forgive them? We forget everything, we get all friendly, we bury our dead? Is that what you're suggesting? Congratulations, really. Congratulations."

"That was all a hundred years ago. Mehmet is not guilty of any of it. He's not a murderer. He hasn't killed anyone."

"I'm happy that you are in love," said Victoria, in a sweeter voice. "You caught us by surprise. Given a little time, perhaps we could…"

"No," Aram interrupted, guessing the end of her sentence. "It's simply impossible."

"Romeo and Juliette, your turn now!" Arthur exclaimed, trying to make a joke that would lighten the atmosphere.

Anoush said nothing. With everyone either furious or in tears, she smiled. In a light-hearted, unexpected tone of voice, she said,

"Come on, don't worry. There is no Romeo. I just made the whole thing up."

"What are you saying?" Aram asked, warily.

"I was just winding you up. There is no Mehmet in my life. I just invented everything so that I could see your reaction."

"I don't understand," *mayrig* said. "What are you playing at? Is this some kind of test of tolerance and understanding?"

"Anoush, that joke is really bad taste. I hope you realize that."

For the first time in his life, Aram was disappointed in his daughter. His precious little girl had angered him, hurt him. Arthur, on the other hand, tried to stand up for his sister. He looked at her and said, "Perhaps you think that history is about moving on. You have to turn the page. And maybe you're right. Is that why you invented Mehmet?"

There was no reply.

"Let's leave him as an imaginary person, then," said their father, relieved yet determined. "He has no place at our table."

By that time, it was getting dark in the dining room. Becca lit some white candles, and, getting up, announced that it was time for dessert.

Two weeks later, Arthur was having a beer with his friend Igor. They were sitting at the Excelsior, a lively bar where they often met to watch soccer. That evening, in an atmosphere that was as charged indoors as out on the field, the Spanish team was playing Argentina. Arthur and Igor had known each other since kindergarten. Arthur appreciated his friend's warm presence: a love of chocolate in any form had given him a stout appearance that he was rather proud of, despite the fashion of the day. Igor liked to laugh loudly, even at himself. The match was almost over, when he pointed at the door. "Look who's here!"

Arthur turned around to see Anoush enter the bar, dressed in a long-sleeved blue dress. She was holding hands with a stranger, a thin young man with dark hair. Arthur made a sign, although she did not reply. She seemed annoyed to see her brother, even giving him the impression that she was about to retrace her steps, but they were too close already to avoid running into each other. The guys came up to her, and as Arthur went to hug her, Anoush pushed her friend forward.

"I'd like you to meet Mehmet."

Arthur glanced at his sister in surprise, but her look said everything: "I'll explain later. Right now, just shut up."

Igor was in an excellent mood because his favorite team had won (the Spanish were really in form that evening). "Let's sit down and order a drink," he said.

He called the bartender over and before anyone else could speak up, they were sitting at a round table at the back of the bistro. Igor tried to start up a lively conversation, fearing that the unexpected arrival of Anoush and her friend would be awkward. He started going on about one of his favorite TV series whose heroine, Ms. Turnip, was none other than his boss. Cassandra Turnip was a Brit who, according to him, was in full existential crisis, and he had a boundless love/hate relationship with her. He joyfully predicted that the day would come when he would have to do away with her. With her incessant orders and endless requests, she was a total hassle to deal with in the daily life of the office. He hastened to add that, unaware of his deadly plans, she praised him to the skies and showered him with compliments in English: "You are a wonderful man, really, you are. What would I do without you?" Igor, who had a real talent for impersonating people, usually held the complete attention of his audience, but under the current circumstances, he could not win anyone over. Anoush and Arthur, lost in thought, were silent; Mehmet was uncomfortable. Disconcerted, Igor enquired, "Why are you guys so serious? Do you want a beer? We deserve it after a win like that!" (You might have thought he had scored the final goal.)

"No thanks, no beer for me," Mehmet said.

"Would you prefer wine?"

"No, thank you. I don't drink alcohol."

"Really? Never?" Igor asked, adding with a smile, "Are you a member of Alcoholics Anonymous?"

"OK, Igor," Anoush said, as if she were scolding a child. "Leave Mehmet alone."

There was no doubt. Arthur had heard the name correctly. This was Mehmet, then. The slender young man with narrow shoulders took off his jacket and put it on the back of the chair. Silence descended on the group. Igor tried to get the conversation going again.

"Where did you meet Anoush?" he asked Mehmet.

"In medical school. We are in the same lab, and we have practice sessions in the Colline Hospital twice a week."

"Ugh, blood and guts? That stuff freaks me out…" Igor said. "And then what will you do? Do you have a job lined up?"

"When I graduate, I'm going back to my country. My parents live in Istanbul."

"Istanbul?"

"Yes, that's where I'm from. It's my town."

Igor had known the Simonian family for a long time, so he understood that he was on dangerous territory. He stopped talking, which never happened, except in the case of extreme embarrassment. Then, he made a brave attempt to change the topic.

"Ah, talking about Ms. Turnip, I forgot the best story of all. OK, last week, she goes and buys a parrot. She pretends that the queen also has a parrot, and since she is a good

British citizen, she imitates her: God save the Queen and the parrot! Obviously, this parrot is not very nice, and while crazy Cassandra is trying to feed it, it bites her…"

They had stopped listening to Igor joking around. Arthur, perplexed, tried to understand what strange game his sister was playing (if indeed it was a game). Anoush's attitude was even more surprising because up until then, she had dutifully followed the path her parents had set before her. She had always stayed in line, respectful and docile. She never failed to call Arthur to order if she thought it necessary. One night, during the restless years of his adolescence, Arthur came back home late, ignoring his curfew. As he tried to creep into the room unnoticed, Anoush was waiting for him, and rose from the darkness in violent reproach: "Are you oblivious, or what? Can't you see how worried we are about you?" An argument ensued, but as Aram and Victoria were fast asleep, they never actually learned about the incident. Arthur was angry with Anoush and was resentful that their parents, along with the active involvement of Becca, had molded his sister into the image of perfection. He was nonetheless very close to her and no feelings of jealousy could separate them for long; at most, there were just misunderstandings.

The match was over, and the post-game show began. Two breathless reporters discussed the results, comparing the goals of players and analyzing their careers and track records over and over. It was possible, but at this stage purely speculative, that the Argentinian goalkeeper could be transferred to a German club for an unbelievable sum of money. Nobody was really interested in the details, but everyone was glued to the screen. That was how they avoided conversation.

When the waiter brought over the bill, Mehmet grabbed it and paid for the drinks. Igor thanked him with a light tap on the shoulder, and announced, relieved, "Friends, it's time for me to get going."

♯

"I think that I have the right to an explanation," Arthur said, pacing up and down his room, holding the phone very close.

"Yes, of course," Anoush replied reluctantly.

"OK, I'm listening."

"Well, let's get one thing straight. You're not a prosecutor, and I'm not on trial. Where do you think we are, a courtroom?"

"I know very well that we're not in a courtroom. We're at home, and you managed to make everyone mad at you by making that stupid announcement on the day of the commemoration."

"It wasn't a stupid announcement. It was the truth."

"Wait a minute. First Mehmet exists, then he doesn't. 'You see, I just made the whole thing up…' And two weeks after that big scene, in you come to the bar holding hands with your fiancé, miraculously brought back to life: 'Hi, I'd like you to meet Mehmet.' What movie are we in?"

Arthur was shouting into the phone, unable to hold himself together.

"If you just calm down, I can tell you what happened."

"Go ahead, I'm listening, but just tell me the truth."

"Arthur, you want the truth? Here it is. I'm in a crappy situation and I don't need any lectures. It's pointless."

"I'm not lecturing you. I'm just giving you my opinion. OK, give me your version of the story."

"Why do you keep talking about *my* version, or *my* point of view? Are you finally going to listen to me?"

Anoush's voice faded away. Arthur imagined his sister in the small apartment that *hayrig* had generously provided for her: she must be stretched out on the beige velvet couch, a present from Becca, purchased one winter morning in the flea market.

"I already told you," Arthur replied. "I'm listening. Go on."

"I've known Mehmet for quite a while. You see, we've got a lot in common, and he's the kindest and most intelligent man I've ever met."

"OK, I understand, he's kind and intelligent, and he's in medical school with you. That doesn't mean you have to marry him, right?"

"Why are you sticking your nose into my business? Why shouldn't I marry him? What's the problem?"

"You know very well what the problem is. Armenia and Turkey are sworn enemies, that's the problem. It's just impossible."

"Impossible? Who says it's impossible? You're just repeating the speech that *hayrig* made…"

"This guy's ancestors eliminated our family."

"Mehmet has nothing to do with that."

"Excuse me, but you can't get rid of the past just because it suits you. That's too easy. Think for a moment. What if Mehmet's grandfather had been holding the knife that killed *our* grandfather? Your young man has blood on his hands, and even if it's symbolic, I couldn't care less. You know that, just as well as you did on the day of the commemoration that you ruined."

"I will not allow you to say that! I didn't want to ruin anything!" said Anoush, raising her voice.

"So why did you lie?"

"When I saw how everyone reacted, I got scared, so I pretended it was just a joke. It was a mistake, I see that, but I never imagined there would be such a fuss. And now I really don't know what to do…"

"But it's easy. Just forget about Mehmet! You can easily find another guy who would be very happy to go out with you."

As he said these words, Arthur knew that he had gone

too far. He heard a click. Anoush had hung up. He called her right back, but it went to voice mail. He sat quietly, uncertain of what to do. What exactly was Anoush guilty of doing, anyway? Why should she be carrying the weight of history? Why did she need to navigate which family ties were and were not allowed? These were no longer the days when parents decided who their children could marry, and there was no longer any need to obey rules that had no legitimacy. So what if Anoush wanted to marry the descendant of an Ottoman? Nobody had the right to stop her. Not even her beloved *hayrig*. Aram Simonian was so profoundly loved that he held a considerable influence over his family. He was regarded as the patriarch. He could be tyrannical and sweet at the same time. But for the first time, his daughter had tried to free herself from his influence.

A moment later, not really knowing what to think, Arthur was having a strong cup of coffee when the phone rang. He thought it would be Anoush, but to his surprise, he saw it was Becca's number at this late hour.

"Arthur," she said, dispensing with the preliminary remarks that she always used, "you must have been angry with your sister when she announced her wedding."

"Of course. Like everyone."

"Even more because she hadn't mentioned anything to you…"

"Yes, right. I was very surprised."

"I understand, but it was just a joke she made up on the spot."

Arthur hesitated. Should he tell Becca that he had just met the phantom fiancé in a bar? But he kept his mouth shut. If he revealed the truth, he would feel that he was betraying his sister.

"Actually," Becca continued, "I was very touched for a reason that I didn't give at the table."

Knowing the eccentricities of dear Becca, he wondered what she was suddenly about to reveal.

"As you know, a wedding announcement is not just a happy occasion. It's also very serious. I had that experience a long time ago, before you were born."

Arthur was astonished. He had always thought that Becca had always been single, fiercely giving priority to her independence and her career as an actress. "Theater is my husband," she would say, "and it will be until the day I die!"

"Were you going to get married?"

"Yes, and like Anoush, I also announced my wedding."

"Don't tell me that you were in love with an Ottoman!"

"No, no, he was German. His name was Ludwig. Actually, his name was Hans Peter, but I called him Ludwig."

"Oh yes? How come?

"He was a musician. He played the violin. Beethoven was his favorite composer, so I nicknamed him Ludwig! And whenever he drove me crazy, which was often, I called him Mr. Van. We had a fitful, even fierce kind of relationship. One day, I was so angry that I almost broke his violin. You can imagine the scene, Arthur! We fought a lot, but it never lasted long. We always made up right away. He would send flowers to the theater, and I'd forgive him on the spot. I was crazy about that man. I breathed with him, I breathed for him. No boundaries, no worries. It was an absolute, delicious, even a destructive feeling."

Then she added, more slowly, "A grave mistake…"

Becca told the story of the wedding announcement. She had invited the entire family to an Italian restaurant, a modest bistro, because they didn't have much money at that time. She chose the place because she loved the Chianti house wine. She knew the waiters, who moonlighted as singers in their off hours. They had sung a Sicilian tune, and then she had made her announcement. Ludwig wasn't there at the time because he was on tour with his orchestra. "A fabulous journey," he said in the last letter he sent, but it was a trip from which, to Becca's despair, he never returned.

"He disappeared? What happened?"

"To this day, I don't really know. In Berlin, he met up with a young woman he had known from before. I don't know if that was by chance or if it had been planned. She was a secretary at a publishing house. He had shown me her photo one time, leaning on a bridge, with a big hat. In his goodbye letter, Ludwig gave me that tired old line: 'I'm really sorry…' And then, nothing. I couldn't believe it. I thought I was going crazy. I thought I couldn't live without him. I was in half a mind to go to Berlin to get him back, by sheer willpower or by force, but your father advised me against it. He said, 'Don't worry. You'll soon find someone else!' (Arthur reacted with a start. Those were the exact words that he himself had used to speak to his sister). Even today, Mr. Van fills me with a heavy heart. I'm still angry, even though many years have gone by. That bastard, he left me…"

Arthur began to empathize with his aunt's emotions when she heard Anoush's announcement. She had not dared take his sister's side that day.

Becca was silent for a moment.

"Forgive me. I'm boring you with my old memories. I needed to air them out a bit, I don't know why…"

He asked Becca why nobody had ever spoken of the violinist, or of his trip and failure to come back.

"You never told us any of this. It's unbelievable! It's high time I learned more about this family's secrets."

"Remember: we're a family of survivors. And do you know the golden rule with survivors?"

"I should know it, but tell me…"

"Rule number 1. No foraging in the past, for fear that you

will get buried beneath it. Rule number 2 (which follows Rule number 1): keep moving forward. A better future awaits you."

And then, without further ado, she added: "It's late, my blue-eyed nephew. Good night!"

On May 29th, Arthur was celebrating his 23rd birthday. Aram invited the family for lunch at *La Mirabelle*, a pretty family restaurant on the edge of the lake. It was a calm place, its walls decorated with oil paintings. The owner, Ms. Andrieu, a woman with scarlet glasses and a lively smile, welcomed her customers at the entrance to the restaurant. When Arthur arrived, she recognized him, and said, "Come on, they're waiting for you. I believe it's your birthday! I've saved you the best table, next to the window." The hostess showed him in, and he saw his parents and Becca, who were all dressed up in his honor. Anoush was not there.

Once her nephew was seated, Becca began rummaging in her bag. She took out a rectangular envelope, brandishing it as if she had found some treasure. "Arthur, here's a little present for you." Becca loved ritual phrases, and 'a little present for you' was one of them; she used it on every important occasion. One Christmas, she forgot to say it, and they all teased her about aging prematurely and losing her memory.

"We're giving him the presents over dessert," Aram said. He loved to be in control. As he spoke, the restaurant menu was passed around and a waiter in a white shirt served them some water.

"Let's order something to drink while we wait for everyone," Aram proposed. "Champagne all around? How about it?"

"I'm just wondering where Anoush is. She should have gotten here at least twenty minutes ago," Victoria said, her eye on the door. At that moment, a group of elderly people came into the restaurant, but Anoush, always on time, was not among them.

"Why don't you call her?" Aram suggested to his son.

Arthur took out his cellphone. He was looking for his sister's number when it started to vibrate, and he saw a new message.

> Arthur,
> Forgive me, I'm going to miss your birthday. Mehmet and I have found a low-cost flight to Vienna. We'll be gone for three days. Make up some excuse for me. I love you a lot.
> Anoush

He read the message twice, thinking that despite the *I love you a lot*, Anoush was asking too much.

"I just got a message from Anoush." (Despite his disappointment, he forced himself to sound as normal as possible.)

"Why is she late?" Aram asked. "When is she getting here?"

"She isn't coming."

"What's going on?" Victoria asked, getting worried. "Why didn't she tell us?"

"I don't think she had time. She got a last-minute ticket to Vienna, a really good deal that she didn't want to miss out on."

"Did she go alone?

Arthur kept his composure.

"No idea. Absolutely no idea."

"Well, one thing is for sure," Becca said, laughing. "She hasn't gone on her honeymoon!"

"You never know…"

Slowly, Arthur was starting to find his sister's attitude unbearable. He felt like revealing the existence of Mehmet.

"Anoush is losing it," Aram said. "I still haven't gotten over that stupid joke she played on us on April 24th."

Then, turning to his son, he asked, "And you? Do you understand what's going on? You and your sister are always in on each other's secrets. The two of you share everything."

"That's not true. We're not even sharing my birthday dinner."

Arthur really wanted to tell them everything, but he resisted the temptation. He felt alone and he had the impression that he was an actor playing his part badly.

"Do you want an explanation?" Becca asked. "Well, it's quite simple. Anoush has always been the perfect daughter and the perfect sister. It's always been very hard. She wants to make her own choices, and stand on her own two feet. Can't you understand how difficult it is to be perfect all the time? A few years ago, I was working with a director who was a perfectionist, and …"

Arthur interrupted his aunt.

"We know, you always stand up for Anoush. If she wants to live her life without worrying about us, that's her right. But she could have…"

"OK, OK, don't take it personally," Becca said, playing with the pearls on her necklace. "I'd like to remind you that we have very high expectations in this family. Perhaps too high."

She shrugged, happy to have expressed an opinion that she had kept to herself for too long, but anxious not to get into a confrontation with her brother.

"It's true, we ask a lot of our children," Aram said, looking for his wife to agree. "And it's normal. We've worked hard for them to have a nice life. Our expectations go hand in hand with the efforts we've made for them."

With a nod, Victoria agreed with *hayrig*. Losing his train of thought for a moment, Arthur cast his mind back to Mehmet and the involuntary role that slim young man had played in this Armenian family. He certainly couldn't have suspected it, unaware of the shadow that the past threw on their present situation.

Arthur spoke to his father. "And you always thought Anoush would rise to your expectations, even more than me. You can say so now."

"It's true, I must admit. But I was wrong."

"You were lucky," Becca said, winking at her nephew.

"Oh yes, how come?"

"Because that way you weren't under so much pressure."

"I would have preferred to be under more pressure. And Anoush would have wanted that, too. We could have shared the weight of it."

"Come on, it's your mother and I who have carried the weight," Aram said, leaning against the table. "It was easy for you."

"Papa, you don't understand. Your history is different from ours. And it will always be like that. You can't do anything about it, and neither can we. So leave your comparisons at the door."

There was a bread basket next to the water jug. Arthur took a piece and put it on his plate. At the neighboring table, a man was commenting on the results of the latest elections, his food getting cold.

"Enough for today," Victoria decided. "We are here to celebrate Arthur's birthday and to enjoy this moment together."

She looked at her son. "You're wearing a nice jacket. It goes well with your eyes."

The slender figure of Ms. Andrieu crossed the restaurant toward the Simonian family table. She wanted to know if they were ready to order. Noticing that Arthur was still holding his phone, she remarked, "What a nice family! Do you want me to take a picture? Let's put the young man in the middle…" The photo appeared on the phone's small screen and Aram squinted at it carefully.

"My son's not smiling. Let's try again."

Harry Koumrouyan

III

All the Words They Haven't Told Me

Arthur had a true affection for his family. And yet, three months after his birthday celebration at *La Mirabelle*, an event that left a vague but enduring imprint on his memory, he decided to make a change. The secrets and silences were becoming harder and harder to bear. Family taboos had relegated Mehmet to a world of shadows, and had pushed all explanations into a distant future. For better or for worse, Arthur nonetheless kept telling himself, "When the truth comes out, the Simonian family will be shattered. I don't want to deal with all their feelings. Let them get on without me!" Arthur's attitude to English had only been half-hearted in the past, but he had casually figured out that if he spoke it better, he would be in a stronger position to find a good job once he finished his degree. He swiftly found a pretext for his departure.

He had no trouble getting Aram to support these plans. His father, generous by nature, was even more big-hearted when it came to paying for his children's education. Some simple online research had been enough to find the name of a school in New York. Arthur registered quickly and the confirmation arrived two hours later. He had been accepted. The only thing he needed was a student visa. The embassy, whose bureaucratic procedures felt like some kind of founding principle, operated in a climate of generalized suspicion. Arthur faced one question after another: What was he going to do in the U.S.? How long for? What financial resources did he have? Had he ever been part of the Communist Party? Had he ever been jailed?

He arrived in New York one August day under a pale sky with a high humidity that blanketed the city in a hazy shroud.

51

To avoid the expense of a taxi, he dragged his suitcases to the train station closest to the airport. He had studied the map in advance, and despite numerous transfers, managed to reach Broadway and West 93rd Street, sweaty but with no hitches, in front of the building where he had found a small apartment. The doorman sat at a desk in the entrance, wearing a uniform with gold buttons. He greeted Arthur. "I'm Orlando." He added some pleasantries, difficult for Arthur to understand because of his accent. Orlando extracted an envelope from a tangle of documents. "Here's the key. Take care not to lose it. The elevator is at the end, on the right."

Arthur got into the elevator at the same time as a young woman with fair hair. She shot him a quick smile, looking apprehensive. They got out on the same floor and went the same way. Arthur realized that their doors were next to one another. She appeared more and more fearful. He wondered if she was afraid of being followed. As a way of reassuring her, he dangled the key to his apartment, and nodded at her. In a low voice, she commented, "Ah, you must be the new neighbor. My name's Linda." Arthur introduced himself and held out his hand. She took it without hesitating.

He opened the door. The apartment was smaller than he had imagined. It was only one room, with a tiny bathroom that you had to step up into. One thing he didn't expect to see was the reproduction of a castle on one of the wall panels, with the invitation to "Visit Scotland!" Arthur was to discover that unless they had a fortune, city dwellers often lived in cramped quarters. He had never seen this before, but he got used to the idea with little difficulty. He also got accustomed to the city's limited, almost promiscuous spaces, which people dealt with by putting up an invisible wall around themselves. "I don't see you; you don't see me."

On the chair, he found some sheets and a duvet. He made the bed, and as he lifted the mattress, he found a tiny cockroach. As he tried to squash it, the insect scarpered away. He remembered a sentence that he had read once before. "Cockroaches are the real property owners in New York. Whether you hunt them down or kill them, they will always come back. They're invincible!" Arthur stretched out on the bed, dazed by the jet lag, and a dreamless sleep carried him off. When he woke up two hours later, groggy and dry mouthed, he got up, looked at the furniture, which only consisted of essential items, and wondered where he was. He glanced at the apartment opposite. Some of the windows were lit up, making the building look like a giant advent calendar. Arthur got up, took a shower, and reached into the bottom of his bag for some shorts. He decided to go out.

Joseph opened his blue notebook.

Now, I have a better understanding of why Arthur left for New York. Nobody had ever explained it to me before. Or perhaps they did it in a very (too?) simple way: "He wanted to learn English." Yes, of course he did, but it wasn't only that... The most surprising thing is that afterwards, he didn't come back to Europe. His temporary visit became permanent. I wonder how that happens. One day, you're abroad (which is no longer completely abroad), and you say, "OK, I'm staying here. I'm going to live here. A voluntary exile." Or perhaps you don't make the decision. You are just afraid of going back, even if you don't admit it. You dare not return. You don't ask the real question: "What if, back home, in my house, I no longer belong? Perhaps they've forgotten me." So you let time go by, thinking that you'll deal with it all later. You might even enjoy this move. You are from everywhere and from nowhere. The Simonian family is used to immigration. In the beginning, it was survival, and then, it became a choice. You have a suitcase, ready, in the corridor. You don't wait to be chased away in order to leave.

Arthur walked up Broadway toward Harlem. The humidity had been replaced by a light breeze, which loosened its damp grasp. A small, noisy crowd went by. A young father, running in big strides as he pushed along his baby's carriage, skirted around a cardboard box with a human shape coiled up inside, heavy and immobile.

A thought suddenly dawned on him. Despite the exhaustion of the trip, he realized that his reality was going to change now that an ocean separated him from his precious but troublesome family. After all, if Anoush married Mehmet, even in secret, the choice was hers to make, and nobody would ask Arthur to resolve the conflict when they found out. Depending on your point of view, this marriage was either scandalous or insignificant. "Stay out of it! This isn't your problem," he repeated to himself, as if he wanted to put it out of his head.

He continued with his walk. Not far from Columbia University, whose imposing buildings stretched along the avenue, he passed under the awning of a theater, and even though the building seemed boarded up, he noticed a shiny sign on a side door: *Elmers School for Performing and Visual Arts*. Approaching, he saw that the school was accepting applications for acting and singing courses until the end of the month. "And why shouldn't I apply?" Arthur asked himself, suddenly inspired. Without a second thought, he realized that it would not take him so long, and that learning to be an actor in another language could be very useful. All he had to do was to talk to Aram, but he imagined his reaction. "Actor! In New York!" It would be as if the association between a life on stage and life in a big city were somehow destructive. "He'll have a meltdown," Arthur thought. He started to formulate the arguments he would use to defend this decision to pursue acting to his father. There were numerous advantages (just as if he were reciting a sentence before a test, he kept repeating forcefully "definitely numerous arguments"). He could improve his accent, read great texts and enrich his vocabulary… It would be good to learn it all. He would tell Becca first. After all, she had been an actress and would give her nephew all the advice he needed. Arthur decided to call her the very next morning.

He heard his name. "Next candidate, please. Arthur Simonian? Is that you?"

Paralyzed, he did not reply immediately, but then he heard the question again. He looked over the appointment letter carefully before he handed it in, just to reassure himself that he hadn't made a mistake with the day or the time. Everything was in order. His audition to the theater school was for the 31st of August, at five o'clock.

He was wearing black pants and a black shirt, as he had been told. His clothes were wrinkled since he didn't know how to iron. He hoped that the interview panel would not notice, or, at least would not hold it against him. The assistant signaled to him as the ice cubes clinked in his cold drink. "The audition is down there. Ms. Laurel and her colleagues are waiting."

Arthur went down the iron staircase. It gave off an acrid smell of bleach, proof of a recent cleaning. He arrived in a small, dark theater that looked more like a well-furnished cave than an auditorium. The walls, painted in a light green color, could have used a clean coat of paint, while the frayed velvet armchairs had seen better days. There was a ceiling fan that looked like a beetle from a distance. It spun slowly round. Emma Laurel sat in the first row. She wore a silk blouse with a violet brooch, and her elegance and authority contrasted with the modesty of the room. To her side, a heavyset man was sprawled on a chair, a laptop perched unsteadily on his knees. There was a young woman in a very short skirt at the end of the row. Emma Laurel gave Arthur an unconvincing smile.

"Welcome, Mr. Simonian. Thank you for your interest in our school. How did you learn about our courses?"

For a moment, Arthur felt disinclined to tell her about the strange turn of affairs that had brought him to this audition, the way he had taken a walk uptown the day he arrived in New York. When he told Becca about his plans, she had broken out in a smile. "My blue-eyed nephew wants to learn acting! He wants to assume a role, perhaps become someone else. Meanwhile, my niece almost marries an Ottoman. This family is definitely crazy!" Arthur made no retort. He just wanted her to give him some tips about how to approach Aram. Becca, never short of ideas, advised him, "Tell him that this theater is part of your language school - that would be the easiest way. If not, there'll be a scene!"

Emma Laurel realized that Arthur had not replied. She repeated, cordially but insistently,

"How did you learn about our theater?"

He avoided the question.

"I know that the school has been around for a long time…"

"Yes, that's right. It was established in 1973 by Olivia

Elmers, a tremendously…" (she underlined that word with a gesture of her right hand) "talented actress. At the end of her career, after she'd played on every stage in the country, she decided to establish a school to promote the arts and share her experience. We are honored to follow in her footsteps."

Before Arthur could reply, Emma continued, "I imagine that you've never heard of Olivia Elmers. You're much too young. This was a woman that could take on any role, but her most famous one was as Blanche DuBois in *Streetcar.*"

"*Streetcar?*" Arthur asked, trying to understand what she was referring to.

"*A Streetcar Named Desire,*" Emma Laurel continued.

The man who was sprawled out on the chair frowned at Arthur. Voluntarily or not, he came to his aid.

"Tennessee Williams' play…"

The candidate looked at the three people who were about to determine his fate. For a minute, he wondered if he was dreaming or if he really was inside a theater in New York. This decision to apply to the school had been made on the spur of the moment. He told himself, "I'll do it. What do I have to lose?"

The man made an awkward movement and dropped the laptop. He swore, while Emma looked on, exasperated.

"Bill, your damned machine holds our entire database. You're so clumsy."

"Don't worry," murmured Bill. "This device is solid."

Turning to Arthur, she added, "I much prefer pencil and paper. I know, I might be the last one left, but so what? What about you, Mr. Simonian?"

Arthur, who had not written anything by hand for several years, gave a vague reply. Emma looked happy enough. She turned toward the young woman in the short skirt.

"Your turn, Mandarine. Go ahead."

"Thank you," said the young woman, whose deep voice

jarred with her frail appearance. Tell us about yourself, Arthur.

The young man was not yet used to being called by his first name, something that Americans did often, so he hesitated a second, as if Mandarine had gotten the wrong person. But he immediately let it go and explained who he was and where he came from. The examiner had a remarkably short attention span. She interrupted Arthur after a few sentences, nodding her head like a teacher who was pleased with a student's reply.

"Very interesting. You can imagine that we are eager to see you on stage. Remind us which passages we sent you."

"I've learned a monologue from *King Lear* and an excerpt from the new play *All the Words They Haven't Told Me.*

"*All the Words They Haven't Told Me!* Great! A brilliant text," said Mandarine, emphatically. "Let's start with that one. The author is adorable, the friend of a friend. She was a total triumph in Chicago, where the play was released last winter. You must have noticed its dramatic shifts."

"Yes," Arthur replied timidly.

"OK, let's go, I'll play the other part."

Mandarine got up and invited Arthur to follow her, turning on the spotlight that would illuminate the stage. Without any props – the set was empty – but with as much conviction as he could muster, the candidate took on the role of Dimitri, a Greek fisherman accused by his unemployed father of robbing him of a large sum of money. *"Never! Believe me, I didn't take a penny. I'm not the scumbag you think I am. You have no proof for your accusations! I'm clean. I know you lost your job. You need that money, but I'm sure you'll find it…"*

The pitch increased as hostility developed between the characters. Insults flew thick and fast, and punches were not far behind. But the son would confess to nothing, and the play, in its heavily naturalist but postmodern tone, left the question of Dimitri's guilt open. Arthur had easily memorized the role while Mandarine, holding the text in her hands, had no difficulty improvising. Although she modified the script as she went along, it was clear that she had a real talent for acting. With her long legs, dressed in a pocket handkerchief that barely covered her body, she effortlessly assumed the role of the father. *"Thief! You've betrayed me, and I can't forgive you. Get on the first boat that arrives, and leave the island. The gods will catch you and punish you."*

Once he had acted out the scene, Arthur sat down again, out of breath as if he had been playing sports. Without permitting him a break, Mandarine stayed on the stage. It was as if she were transformed into a predator, fixed on her prey.

"So, what do you think? Did Dimitri steal his father's money? What do you believe we can assume?"

Arthur hesitated.

"Well, the play doesn't say. It's up to the audience to decide."

"Of course, but the actor is going to try and share his understanding of the text, to give the audience his own view of the story. It's fundamental to his performance, wouldn't you say? You have to decide what you're going to make of Dimitri: is he an untrustworthy son, or a victim?"

"Well, I'll wait for instructions from the director. The band leader chooses the tempo," Arthur replied, acting like a good student. "And then, the actors will work together. First they'll read the play to understand the story, especially the sub plot, and all the words the characters don't tell you. They…"

"I need you to respond directly to the question. I'm not looking for some watered-down answer," Mandarine interrupted. "It's *your* reading that interests me. That's what counts!"

Arthur was silent. He was exhausted by the exercise, and had switched off. Without wanting to, he had allowed his own life to get mixed up with the text. He had become the Greek fisherman, and Aram, like a shadow puppet, had appeared on the stage, a secret guest whose familiarity both reassured and accused him. He seemed to reproach his son for having fled to New York, sought refuge, played the role of an ambiguous character who, yes, had perhaps stolen from his own father. In Arthur's mind, *All the Words They Haven't Told Me* had escaped from the playbill to his own mind, taking on the feeling of guilt that tormented him.

Passing a delicate finger over her violet brooch as if she wanted to make sure it was properly fastened, Emma Laurel congratulated Arthur on his correct pronunciation since after all, he was not a native speaker. She thanked him and told him that the audition was over. Shortly, he would be informed if he had been admitted.

On the telephone, he clearly heard Becca's voice.

"So, the audition?"

"Tough…"

"Of course! It's an entrance exam. What role did you play?"

"I was Dimitri, a Greek fisherman, suspected by his father of having robbed him."

"Ugh, that's awful," laughed Becca. "So, is the rascal guilty, or not?"

"We don't know. The author left the ending open."

"Great, so you're not the prisoner of the story. You can choose. Those are the best roles, the ones that you can fashion as you like."

"You sound like Mandarine."

"Mandarine?"

"She was a member of the panel. A thin young woman, in a short skirt. She played the other part."

"Did she help you?"

"Not really. She deviated from the script whenever she felt like it."

"Oh, I see… People want to test the candidates' reactions. That's an old trick. Did you get on OK?"

"No, it really threw me off course."

"Off course, during an audition? That's not a good sign."

"I know, I know, but you can't control these things. *Hayrig* made an unexpected appearance on the stage…"

"Aram?" Becca interrupted. "The ghost that appears unsummoned from the wings… Don't tell me that he showed up in the middle of the play!"

"Yes, all of a sudden he was right there in front of me."

"Listen to me, my little nephew. Theater is inspired by life, but it's not real. Leave Aram where he is. He hasn't rowed over to see you, or taken a supersonic plane across the Atlantic, has he?"

"Not that I know of," said Arthur, a smile appearing on his face.

"Another thing. You didn't tell me the name of the play."

"All the Words They Haven't Told Me."

"Nice title! Now, I have a better understanding of why your father took part in the audition."

"Oh yes? Explain that to me."

"It's simple," Becca said, a little solemnly. "In this crazy family, the things we want to say are often cloaked in silence."

Arthur wanted to switch topics. So he asked,

"What about you? Do you remember some of your own auditions?"

"Now that I'm not acting any more, I've forgotten quite a lot of things, especially all the times I was turned down for a part! I do remember one Canadian play. I was playing the role of Helen Clark, a fifty-year-old woman whose husband leaves her, even though she thinks they have a stable relationship. One summer evening, in the garden of their country house, they're sipping on a glass of wine when suddenly the guy announces to Helen that he doesn't love her anymore and that he's leaving. It's a shock for her, because she doesn't expect it. You know, the classic scenario… On the day of the audition, I asked to play the scene twice, so as to give two different interpretations of the character. I repeated the exact same words, even the most mundane ones: *"Leave. You've betrayed me. I never want to see you again."* Helen could act destroyed, she could plead with him or be furious, or she could be split between sadness and pride. I really wanted to convince the director to give me the role. And I succeeded. They took me on, and the play was a big success. They put it on again a few years later and it was translated into several languages. It's a universal theme, so it travels well!"

That thought made them both laugh, and the conversation ended. Arthur took a beer out of the small refrigerator built into the wall next to the sink and the water heater. He took a swig, spread out on the bed and half dozed off. He was thinking of Dimitri, the Greek fisherman, and Helen Clark, the humiliated wife, when he thought he heard someone softly crying. Convinced that he'd been dreaming, he told himself: "All the words they haven't told me, but all the tears that you can hear…" The sound stopped, and then came back. He listened closely. Behind the wall, in the apartment occupied by the young woman he had met the day he arrived, someone was crying. He waited for a few moments, then got up and stepped out of his apartment. He hesitated for a moment in the deserted hallway before knocking on Linda's door. Nobody replied. Was it tactless to knock again? He said: "It's Arthur, your neighbor. Arthur

Simonian. Is everything OK? Tell me if I can help you at all…"

The sobs receded, first replaced by complete silence, and then by the click of a lock. Held back by the safety lock, the door only cracked open a few centimeters. Linda Wells appeared, her face red and streaked with tears. She was barefoot. "Oh, it's so nice of you to bother. Thank you, but everything is OK." She repeated, in a whisper: "It's OK…"

Through the gap, Arthur could see a small sofa. A pair of yellow high-heeled shoes had been thrown on the floor, evening shoes that could perhaps transform this young woman with wet eyes into a princess. On the wall opposite the door, Arthur saw a poster of an island. There was a beach with parasols on the edge of a wide bay. It must be the Caribbean. Linda added, "I'm sorry if I disturbed you. You can hear everything in this building. I'm not used to these paper-thin walls. I used to live in a house. That's when I still lived with my parents…"

Linda unfastened the security chain. She kept her hand on the doorknob, and Arthur stayed at the entrance.

"Tell me your name again. I'm sorry, I didn't catch it."

"Arthur Simonian."

"Simonian?"

"That's right. It's an Armenian name."

Linda looked inquisitive, but she didn't ask any more questions. She added:

"Well, my last name is Wells. Actually, my father's father came from Poland and his name was Kaczonowski. When he got here, the immigration official made fun of him and said he would baptize him Wells. He said, 'Kaczonowski, nobody will have any idea! You'll spend your whole life spelling out your name. What do you think of Wells?' My grandfather couldn't understand a word, and he accepted it without question. He must have been scared that he would be sent back. But me, I'd prefer to have a

Polish name. Linda Wells, it's so common. In this country, thousands of people have that name. If I close my eyes, I see all those Linda Wells lined up: fat ones, old ones, thin ones… and me. It makes me dizzy. Do you understand? The day I become famous, I'm going to call myself Linda Kaczonowski, and too bad if people don't know how to spell it!"

"Would you like to be famous?"

"Yes, because I like singing. And I like to sing for other people. In a month's time, I'm going to enter a competition."

Without skipping a beat, Linda Wells struck up some lines of a popular song, but she didn't know the words well. When she couldn't remember them, she made something up instead. Once she finished, Arthur smiled. He took his leave. "I wonder why she was crying," he said. "She's so pretty. I can imagine her wearing her yellow shoes…"

One bright September morning, Arthur ran into the mail carrier in the lobby, and was handed an envelope. He recognized the name of the theater school in the left-hand corner, and opened the letter. "Dear candidate, we are sorry to tell you…" He was really disappointed, and he hid it from Linda Wells, who came in at that moment. She placed her hand on his shoulder by way of greeting, and suggested that they go to see the first roses that had come out in Central Park. "We have to go quickly," she said. "They'll soon wither and die."

He followed Linda, and ten minutes later, they were on the Great Lawn of Central Park. People of all ages were running along the reservoir, and behind the curtain of elms and oaks, you could see the façades of the tall buildings along 5th Avenue. Linda Wells lifted her head up to the sky.

"Look at that intense blue color. That's the color of New York. The color of the sky on September 11th 2001."

Harry Koumrouyan

IV

An Unexpected Guest

There were several months of chaos, tantrums, tears and reconciliations when the Simonian family finally learned that the Ottoman fiancé actually did exist. And then, that chapter came to an unexpected end. Anoush did not marry Mehmet after all. Unlike the theatrics that had accompanied her marriage announcement on April 24th, there was a sense of sobriety when Anoush informed her family, almost in passing, about the breakup. She refused to give the least explanation, so there were none of the details that the family expected to hear. Of course, they were all eager to know why the young man was no longer on the scene ("What could possibly have happened? Did he leave her? Or did she finally admit that the relationship was going nowhere?"). The questions were short lived, however, because everyone was so relieved that the whole thing was over. What remained difficult to untangle was the knot of intertwined sincerity and provocation, but Anoush's final words quashed all possible discussion: "Mehmet's going back to Istanbul." Her parents concealed their delight, but Becca was less discreet. She took her niece on a trip to the Alps, believing that altitude is the best thing to settle someone down. Unfortunately, she didn't entirely attain her goal. Anoush had given up the role of the perfect young woman she had played before Mehmet appeared in her life. Having managed to assert herself, she was no longer afraid of confronting Aram and Victoria over sensitive topics like the drama, the past, their origins. Even though the family was navigating calmer waters since the young Ottoman had left, Anoush now wanted to establish her independence in a more definitive way. She decided to give up her Armenian name and to be called Anne from there on out, but she did not break this news to her parents right away. They were the last to know.

As expected, she finished her medical studies with distinction. Aram was filled with pride, and immediately asked her for a photocopy of her diploma. He wanted to hang the precious document on the wall of the office in his jewelry store downtown. Anne tried to dissuade him, but he insisted so vehemently that she eventually let him have his way.

Once she had left school, Anne found a position as auxiliary physician at a clinic in town, and when she was on duty one afternoon, she heard the approaching wail of an ambulance siren. A few moments later, a vehicle drew up outside Emergency, and two nurses pulled out a stretcher carrying a young man, only semi-conscious. It was a cyclist, run over by a speeding car. Anne checked his injuries, taking his blood pressure and pulse. Later that evening, she was reassured to find that the accident was less serious than originally feared. When the patient came to, he told her that his name was Eric Landolt and that he was a lawyer.

"And what is your name, if I may?"

Anne showed him the badge on her blouse. Her name was written in small letters.

"Doctor Simonian. Anne Simonian."

"Are you Armenian?"

"Yes, my family is. I was born in Geneva."

"So, Dr. Simonian, could you discharge me now? I think I'm doing better."

Anoush hesitated for a moment, but she thought it was advisable for the patient to spend the night. She called the duty nurse, who wheeled the patient into a room where an older man was asleep. Eric also fell asleep quickly, and was able to leave the hospital the next day after breakfast.

A few days later, Eric Landolt came back for a checkup, and was happy to see Anoush again. She cleaned the wound (a deep gash on his thigh) and changed the dressing. The young man watched the skill with which she managed each movement. "She's young, but she seems to have a lot of experience," he thought.

"Your wounds have healed quickly, Mr. Landolt."

"I'm a quality product," he laughed. It's my parents that you should compliment!"

"I'll happily do that, if I ever meet them. Did you tell them about the accident?"

(Anne learned that the patient's family lived in Zurich, that he had grown up in a house on the more affluent side of the lake. He was an only child. His grandfather was a financier and his mother collected paintings.)

"The next dressing will be lighter, and you can change it yourself."

"Are you abandoning your patient? Well, maybe we can meet up for coffee. What do you think?"

As he spoke, Anne noticed his straight, white teeth. They were perfectly aligned, and this seemed to give him a swaggering appearance.

She gladly accepted the invitation, surprising even herself. The following Saturday, she met up with Eric at a small bistro near the clinic. They stayed there for two hours: no one else was around. Eric told her about his childhood.

"I lived in a bubble, protected from the world's realities. But at some point, I needed to get out and see something different. My parents didn't understand that, and they tried to make me change my mind."

Anoush didn't think it was a good moment to explain how deeply she understood. She could see why he needed to leave his closest family circle. She thought about how her brother had left for New York.

"You were scared of suffocating."

"Exactly! Very insightful, doctor!" He added, "Look, we

can use the *tu* form, I mean, address each other less formally, if you like…"

There were other meetings after this one. Anoush was seduced by Eric's vivacity and humor: he always seemed at ease in any situation. But he made her wary by wanting to see her all the time. It was as if the episode with Mehmet had made her more cautious. At the movies one evening, Eric put his arm around her shoulder, but she pushed him away, muttering ambiguously that he should wait. The next time they met, Eric went back to Anne's apartment after they had had dinner at an Italian restaurant. "Do you want a drink?" she asked. They sat side by side on the velvet sofa that Becca had given her niece. Neither of them said anything, but then Eric turned toward Anoush and gently kissed her. "I prefer to take it slow. You have to understand that," she said. She added no further explanation, not wanting to get into her Ottoman engagement and the way it had ended. Eric would not need to learn about Mehmet until much later.

After a year in which the relationship grew in intensity and involvement, Eric asked Anoush to marry him. This time, the marriage announcement did not cause a scandal in the Simonian family. On one hand, the fiancé was what used to be called 'a good catch'; on the other, the Ottoman episode, once over, had somehow allowed *hayrig* and *mayrig* to envisage a different kind of family. Only Becca was hesitant with respect to the young lawyer. Although he seemed so perfect, she gave no reason for her opinion. For their part, Eric's parents welcomed the newcomer with a combination of reservation, warmth, and respect toward her. Anne didn't feel completely at ease in their swanky home. Eric's mother presented the young woman with a jewelry case covered in pale silk. She explained, "I'd like to give you something. This belonged to my great grandmother." Anoush opened the small parcel and found the prettiest piece of jewelry she had ever seen. It was a brooch, embossed with amethysts, that had been passed down from one generation to the next. In the Simonian family, this would never have been possible because the massacres and then exodus had not only killed human beings, but destroyed their possessions as well. "We have nothing from those times," Aram would state sadly. "Nothing at all."

The wedding took place at a church in the countryside, and Mendelssohn's Wedding March accompanied the newlyweds out of the church, to great applause from the crowd. In the gardens of a nearby hotel, a sumptuous feast was laid out, together with a bar, which was set up around a fresh water pond bordered by beds of oleander. The waiters wore cream-colored gloves and black vests. They glided from one guest to the next, pouring champagne and offering hors d'oeuvres of foie gras. Anne's friends were dressed in elegant attire, while Eric's companions laughed loudly, their lips wet with alcohol. A professional photographer followed the couple diligently around, and went from one group to another, leaning in and out to get the best shots. Aram, proud as ever, motioned them over. The Simonian family struck a pose under a cedar tree with lamps strung around the branches. Anne and Arthur, shoulder to shoulder, were squatting in front, and behind them were their parents, Aunt Becca, and Uncle Kevork, who had unexpectedly arrived from Brazil the night before. Kevork had hastily been given a suit and tie. The clothes, which were too big for him, accentuated his slender figure, making him look like a badly dressed actor. The photographer took some shots. They were all bathed in the intense light of that summer day. It looked as if they had been overexposed by a white filter.

Joseph wrote:

We always wonder how our parents met. What I know is that my father had a bicycle and when he was hit by an aggressive driver, my mother took care of him. They met up again for coffee, and, a year later, my father proposed to her. Sometimes they explain, "We met by accident." Really! (Does that make me an accident too, then?) Their wedding photo is displayed on a side table in the living room. It's a little bit out of focus, but I like looking at it anyway because my parents look so good and they are smiling in a way that I have almost never seen them do in real life.

My mother-mom-Anoush-Anne, now I don't really know what to call her, has never told me about Mehmet, or perhaps she mentioned him so quickly that I didn't give him a second thought. It's worthless to ask her any questions: she won't reply. Anyway, I've never really wanted to know. Who cares about her Ottoman? Except…

Ten years earlier, Kevork Simonian, Aram's older brother, had left Europe without telling anyone and moved to an isolated spot in the Amazon rainforest in Brazil. On rare occasions, he sent a brief news update, but he had never given anyone the chance to meet up with him or even see where he was on a map. He disappeared like a specter who had left the land of the living but was not yet dead.

In its immensity, the forest offered Kevork the protection and isolation he sought. Short on resources, he had joined a group of smugglers running drugs between Brazil and Colombia. When he was put in contact with the head of the network shortly after arriving, no questions were asked. This was a lawless world; the past had been effaced and the future did not exist. The men were anonymous. They lived a precarious existence in the here and now. Their business motto was simple: "Do your work and shut up, or else…" Kevork was given a position at the helm of a speedboat. Some white powder was concealed below deck, and he was in charge of transporting it along the river. The boat split the river in a jet of foam.

The trip was dangerous. Several of the transporters had been killed by the military police, who didn't hesitate to pocket the proceeds themselves when they could. Trying to control his fear, Kevork suppressed his true feelings.

One evening, when Kevork had docked on the Brazilian side of the Amazon and was heading down a muddy path into the forest, two men emerged from the shadows and, without saying a word, pointed at the bag slung across his left shoulder. He was seized by terror, but refused to give up his profitable cargo. He knew that the head of the network, a stocky Venezuelan called Jorge, would not believe that the drugs had been stolen once he learned of the attack. He would not hesitate to kill off a disloyal transporter. Kevork was thrown violently to the ground, hitting his head on a stone and losing consciousness. Later, when he came to and examined his face, he could feel the dried blood around his mouth. A yellow parrot observed this injured man shivering with fever. Night had fallen. A band of indigenous people found him and assisted him, administering a local remedy with powerful medicinal effects, which stemmed the infection and saved his life. Kevork stayed in the village of these native people for two weeks, stretched out on a hammock. A series of terrifying nightmares left him breathless. He felt like a swimmer in great danger, hauling himself from the waves. His memories passed before his eyes.

He saw the grey walls of the orphanage where he had taken refuge with Aram after they lost their parents in the Ottoman massacres. The administrator, Carl Stevens, was an American with an imposing stature. An ex-basketball player, originally from Kansas, he approached his wards with two absolute convictions. First, he held firm Baptist beliefs, and second, he believed in the regular and rigorous practice of sport. Besides, beyond the shadow of a doubt, one truth was paramount: God wanted people to take care of their bodies in order to serve Him better. At daybreak, Carl would come into the dormitories, sound Reveille, and force the students to get up and run five laps around the walls of the institution. When they had done this and recited a jumbled murmur of prayers, they ate breakfast, which consisted of bread with a bowl of clear broth. This was served in the refectory by Helga Stevens, who scuttled behind her tank of a husband like a little grey mouse. "Poor, we are so poor…" she would repeat over and over. Kevork would remember this phrase for a long time.

The children were often taken to the municipal pool, where their skin turned red in the icy water. Despite the cold, they had to prove that they could swim faster than the time before. Carl Stevens would stand at the edge of the pool, and in his nasal voice, would shout (always in English), "Faster, faster!" Aram, who was well-built, easily crossed the length of the pool, while Kevork, pallid and thin, struggled along behind him. At the end of the exercise, Stevens would dole out praise and criticism. He never hesitated to malign the slower swimmers. "Kevork Simonian, aren't you older than your brother?" he would ask over and over again. "I can't believe it. Get back in the water and show us that you can do better. Come on, in you get!" It was beyond humiliation. Kevork, his skin wrinkled, was alone in the pool under the mocking gaze of the other children. Aram was the only one darting his brother discreet looks of encouragement. But one day, the jeering was sharper than usual. When Aram saw the tears in his brother's eyes, he clutched his fists, and unable to intervene, spat on the ground. It only took Carl Stevens a matter of seconds to grab the boy by the arm and give him a sharp slap with the back of his hand. It left a mark for several hours.

Once a month, the boys were allowed out for a day. Kevork and Aram would leave the orphanage and go to the nearest town, where they'd meet up with their little sister Becca. She was staying with a couple from Geneva, who, having managed to survive the Ottoman catastrophe, had taken her in. Catherine and Louis Martin had no children themselves, and were stunned by how easily the young orphan learned French. They found a yellowing copy of *Good Little Girls* by the Countess of Ségur in the back room of a bookstore. There were works from all over the world strewn around. Surprised to find this book, which had captivated her as a young girl, Catherine Martin bought it for her young protégée. Becca was entranced. She loved to take refuge in the Château of Camille de Fleurville. This France of the distant past was at her fingertips, inhabited by a picture-perfect heroine. The fury of war and of misery had not reached it. By a strange twist of fate, many years later Becca would act in a satirical play that poked fun at the Countess of Ségur, a work that shone a light on the violence of such a deceptively calm universe. But when she first encountered the novel, Becca never tired of reading it. She yearned to find out more about the characters and their misadventures. Every episode in the book had an impact on her: Sophie Fichini and her foolish mistakes, Sophie's mother who reproached and slapped "her fat, triumphant, spotty, red" daughter whose "lilac silk robe had three large frills," and the dark room where the disobedient girl was locked up.

Thanks to an unexpected inheritance, Louis and Catherine Martin were able to go back to Europe, and they decided to adopt the three young orphans, who kept their family name nonetheless. So, one July morning, Kevork, Aram and Becca Simonian embarked on a ship with their guardians, and sailed from Izmir to Marseille. Leaning on the rail, the transfixed children watched the coast recede into the distance. They could not drag their eyes away from the cruel place where their parents had been killed. They would never return there. After a long interlude, the shoreline flattened into a fine line on the horizon, and then disappeared. Above the ship, the seagulls squawked as they circled above.

When Kevork regained his strength, he prepared to leave the group of Indians who had taken him in. They presented him with a long knife as a goodbye present. It was at that moment that Kevork decided to go back to Europe. He dreaded this difficult decision because he and his family had grown so far apart. Plus, he had never told them anything about his life in the Amazon. He was so apprehensive that he did not alert them that he was going back. He thought of Aram and Becca. "They have their lives, and I have nothing. They are going to ask me questions, want to know everything, and I have nothing to tell them. Or maybe I do! I might have things to say, but that would only frighten them. Why should I even see them again? They'll turn me away, and I'll have to leave…" Even though he was the oldest, Kevork had always had the impression that he was the fragile young brother, crushed by Aram's success and Becca's career. His brother's jewelry store had made him into a wealthy man, and his sister's artistic achievements were regularly featured in the papers. No negative comments had ever been leveled against Kevork, but he believed his siblings had a certain image of him, and he had internalized this persona. Unable to bear it, he had exiled himself on a different continent.

Now he was back, thin and pale, leaning against the window pane in a taxi to Aram's house. Before it got to town, the car drove through a field of sunflowers, and Kevork asked the driver to stop. He took out the knife that the Indians had given him, and cut five flowers, slicing through their thick stems. That would be his welcome present. The taxi started up again. "Are you home for a vacation?" the driver asked. Kevork swallowed and replied, "No, no. I've been living abroad. Ten years in Brazil." The man nodded approvingly and accelerated. It was a small town, and they quickly found their way. Kevork stepped out of the taxi, holding his small suitcase in one hand, and in the other, the black and yellow sunflowers. There before him was the fancy building where his brother and family lived. "I'd better turn back," he thought. "Nobody is expecting me." He lifted his gaze, trying unsuccessfully to peer through the windows. As he was counting the floors, he tripped on the edge of the sidewalk and stumbled, dropping the flowers, which lost some petals. He picked the bouquet back up, and stepped away. Not daring to go in, he circled aimlessly. There was a poorly lit café on the corner of the next street. After hesitating a moment, he sat outside and ordered some wine. The waitress was a young redhead with a Slavic accent. "Ah, you've brought me some sunflowers. That was nice of you!" she said cheekily. But then she added, "Just so you know, we're about to close." Kevork drank his wine, finding that the alcohol had a calming effect. The night spread gently over the town, and he decided that it was time to go to his brother's house. When he got to the door, he heard a hubbub in the apartment, with happy laughter and exclamations. "They're having a celebration…" He stepped back before approaching the door, intimidated, then slowly placed his index finger on the buzzer. This simple gesture suddenly took on so much significance. He pressed the button, but nobody answered. He was tempted to run away, but he controlled himself and rang again. He heard some steps, then the dry click of the lock. Anoush, wearing her wedding dress, appeared before the pink curtain at the entrance. They looked at each other, so stunned that they were unable to say a word. In other circumstances, the scene of this improbable duo would have been comical: Kevork in his sad clothes, crumpled after hours on the plane, and Anoush in her delicate white dress. While Kevork waited awkwardly at the entrance, his niece pulled the bustle toward her, and then, without inviting him inside, turned into the apartment and shouted:

"*Hayrig*, come immediately!"

"What's going on?" Aram asked, without moving.

"Come here. There's a surprise for you."

Now face to face, the two brothers didn't move. Aram slowly approached Kevork and pulled him close. Then he gently pushed him away, looked him up and down, and said, in a matter-of-fact tone of voice:

"You've lost a lot of weight. Are you sick?"

"Sick? No, no, but I'm tired. I've had a long trip."

"Did you come from Brazil? If you'd told us, we would have gone to the airport to pick you up. Why didn't you say anything? Oh, Kevork, with you, we never know. Come on in, the whole family is here. Anoush is getting married tomorrow, and she's trying on her dress. It still needs some alterations. It feels like a tailor's shop inside."

"I'm sorry, I've arrived at a bad moment… I could come back some other time."

"No, not at all. I'm not letting you disappear again. Leave your suitcase here and give me the flowers. Follow me," Aram ordered him.

They went into the living room. When Becca saw her brother, she screamed. She crossed herself as if she had seen a ghost.

"Have you finally decided to come back to Europe?" she asked, without getting up from the armchair. "It's been so long since we heard from you! We'd almost forgotten you. We didn't know how to reach you, and you never gave us your address. We thought you were dead."

"Dead? No, not yet. I was hurt some time ago, but now I'm doing better."

"Did you have an accident? You've chipped your front tooth," Becca said, pointing at her brother's mouth. "What happened?"

Kevork looked down at the Persian rug covering the floor, staring at the red scrolls. They looked like a maze and he wished he could get lost inside it. *Mayrig* pulled carefully at some threads and used dressmakers' scissors to fix a ribbon on the bride's hat, while Anoush and Arthur, sitting side by side in a corner of the room, said nothing. A thick tension had invaded the room with the arrival of their uncle. He had appeared out of the clear blue sky.

"No, I didn't have an accident," Kevork finally replied.

"So what then? Did someone attack you?" Aram asked with a concern he had not shown until then. "Tell us…"

Aram's apprehension finally moved Kevork to speak. With a bravery that shy people sometimes manage to muster, he began to give them a full description of his life in the Amazon. First, he talked about the magnificent landscape, with its humidity and abundant cover of trees. He listed the animals that could only be heard at night, even though they couldn't be seen. Little by little, he started to tell them about the darker details in his life, the business he had gotten into, the dangerous trips along the river, the stupid risks he had taken. Kevork talked for a long time. He was absorbed by the story, and told them every detail, even the most sordid. Sometimes, his voice broke up under the emotion, as if his words gave the truth even more weight. He would interrupt his confession, but after a moment, begin again. Some drops of saliva dripped down his chin. The Simonian family listened to him in a petrified silence. When he stopped talking, Aram got up from the armchair, incredulous and overwhelmed. He went over to his brother, and grabbed him by the arm.

"You're completely crazy!" he shouted. "You've risked your life over and over again. It's a miracle that you're here. What were you looking for in that jungle? Oh, I know, you wanted to escape. But we didn't do anything to you. We never asked you to leave. We would have liked you to stay here with us."

"Aram's right," Becca said. "We're living in Geneva, which is our refuge, our safe place. There's no reason to flee anywhere else, unless it's a voluntary exile. Or, worse, a daredevil adventure. What, you took yourself for a bigshot?"

Kevork didn't answer. His throat was dry, and he was overcome by weakness. He was no bigshot. He was the skinny swimmer in the pool at the orphanage, ridiculed by the giant Carl Stevens.

"Why did you choose that life?" Aram asked. "A taste for danger? The forbidden fruit? Perhaps you thought that you were invincible…"

Still in her wedding dress, Anoush struggled to hear this shocking conversation, which was becoming louder and more tense by the moment. Her joyful celebration had turned into a real scene. And yet, she didn't let Kevork's confession bother her. "Finally," she thought, "he's had the courage to find us and tell us his story. Is it up to us to judge him? A family is not a jury. Kevork has certainly gone off the rails, but, after all, the most plain and respectable men are sometimes the most dangerous."

Arthur decided to intervene. He turned to his father and reprimanded him for speaking to his brother so harshly:

"Hayrig, stop it now. We have to be a bit more understanding. You've made your life here, and you've found your home base. You work hard, there's no doubt about that, but admit it, you've also been lucky. Fate and good fortune have smiled on you..."

Then he looked at Becca.

"And you were lucky too, right? You're a good actress, we know, but that's not enough. When you met that newspaper critic, Charles Lamont, he took you under his wing and sent reference letters to all the theater directors on your behalf. If not, perhaps you would have been stranded by the wayside!"

Aram was taken aback by his son's assertiveness since he was usually more restrained. But after a moment of surprise, he thought, "Arthur's right. He's being logical, my son. I have to calm down." He turned to Kevork and said,

"Come on, let's find you a suit for the wedding. You'll need a tie, too."

The sunflowers were left on the table. They began to droop.

Harry Koumrouyan

V

The Queen of Armenia

It was still hot in New York at night. When he couldn't
sleep, Arthur would push his clammy sheets aside, lean
over the sink, and splash cool water on his face. He'd
stand at the window in the dark, his eyes glued to the
building opposite. He had noticed an apartment midway up
the building where you could see into the living room. It was
sparsely furnished, but there were some unusual pieces
brightly lit up by the lamps. A tall, slender woman seemed
to be the sole occupant. Her face was framed by a full head
of hair. Wearing a closely fitting dress, she sometimes ran
from one end of the room to the other as if seized by an
extreme urgency. She looked like an animal caught in the
headlights of an oncoming car. There were other times when
she sat up perfectly straight in a leather armchair, almost
rigid, absorbed in her reading. The only thing that moved
were her fingers, as she turned the pages of her book with a
minimum amount of effort. Sheltered from the humidity of
the night, Arthur discreetly observed his neighbor, like a spy
trailing a lead. He imagined the occupant on the other side
of the street, this strange woman who never slept, to be the
Queen of Armenia. "She is a sovereign in exile who fled her
country when an earthquake destroyed her castle," he
thought. He imagined her as having an eagle's nest fortress
in the foothills of the Caucasus Mountains. The Queen of
Armenia had roamed the world for some months, and had
then found refuge in America, in this white apartment on 93rd
Street, that Arthur would avidly scrutinize late into the night.
He would stay up, motionless, fearing he would be
discovered. Were that to happen, the woman in the purple
dress would certainly draw the curtains, depriving the young

83

man of his nocturnal rendezvous.

Arthur was disappointed, of course, to be turned down by the acting school where he had applied. But he began to take literature and language courses with Elvira Clusky instead. Like many other American professors, she had transformed her living room into an informal study hall. While she taught, standing against the door frame, the students were asked to sit on ornate chairs with bright yellow cushions. They all did this, except for one Japanese student, who preferred to sit on the floor. On a side table, there was a pot of weak coffee and some blueberry muffins, generously made by Elvira herself. The young woman had just published *The Arsonist,* a novel that had won the attention of critics and earned her several radio and television interviews. "My book is a work of fiction," Elvira would insist. "It is not based on real life, not even remotely. It's just a novel, I assure you!" The reviewers were skeptical, and often rolled their eyes at this declaration, as if they doubted the novelist's own imagination when it came to creating such a dangerous protagonist. *The Arsonist* featured a young pyromaniac that the police were unable to capture. Arthur had bought the book and asked Elvira to write a dedication, which she had willingly done. He was eager to discover this tale of fire and death, whose creator he met every day. Apparently, there was no link at all, at least none that he could deduce, between the smiling, gentle Elvira Clusky and her dark, disturbing novel. "She and her character," Arthur thought, "are the duo from hell, polar opposites who attract one another. I wonder where she found her pyromaniac. Where was he hiding before she found him? He used to be harmless. And yet she brought him out of the shadows and revealed his madness."

Joseph recalled:

When my mother and I went to New York, Arthur showed us Elvira Clusky's novel, carefully shelved on the bookcase. "You should read this book," he told me, "It's impossible to put down once you've started." True, no doubt, but I think that Arthur had a soft spot for Elvira. She was so pretty, yet she'd created a monster! I think he was fascinated by that, even more than by the book itself. Sometimes, Arthur went out of his mind. He thought that the Queen of Armenia lived on the other side of the street… He showed us the floor her apartment was on. It was difficult to imagine, because the apartment looked empty. Mom listened carefully to her brother, as if she knew the story of the Queen. The two of them, Anoush and Arthur, are so close that they seem like twins. Often, they don't even need to speak in order to understand one another, and if they fight, they're quick to make up. And then the cycle begins again.

That Wednesday, Arthur was just getting back from his class when, turning the key, he heard the telephone. He picked up, and heard a young woman's voice.

"Brian, is that you?"

"No, sorry," he said. "It's the wrong number."

"Stop fooling around," the voice retorted. "I recognize you… I know it's you. Answer me."

"You have a wrong number, I'm telling you."

"Come on, are you joking? I know your number by heart."

"Sorry, you…"

"Look, I get it. I know it's you, and you don't want

to talk to me anymore. You don't dare! You may have decided to leave me, but I'm not going to let you go. Never! Do you understand?"

The woman's outburst was a mixture of threat and despair. Arthur was taken aback, but he did not want to interrupt. She was clearly distressed.

"I've only been living in this apartment for a few days, and I'm sure the message on the answering machine hasn't been changed," he stated calmly. "If he ever did live here, the guy you're talking about has left."

"What do you mean? Brian never told me that he was leaving! He would have warned me. Brian always pays close attention to me. I'm really surprised he hasn't been in touch. Something bad must have happened. I'm sure of it."

Arthur tried to reassure her.

"Don't worry, it's probably nothing. Don't you have his cellphone number?"

"No, no, he's not really like other people, he doesn't want a cell phone. He's the only person I know without one, that's him. Look, do you think you could help me find Brian?" asked the woman fervently. "If he shows up, please tell him that I'm looking for him."

"Oh ... well OK, I'll tell him. Sorry... what's your name?"

The woman seemed taken aback.

"My name? How come? Just tell Brian that I've called. He'll know who I am, you can be sure of that." And then, in a suddenly modest tone, she added, "I have to go. I've taken far too much of your time."

Disconcerted, Arthur put the phone back on the hook. That evening, the apartment opposite remained dark. Arthur waited at his post, half fearing that the woman in the purple dress had vanished for good. Disappointed, he was about to abandon this eccentric surveillance when suddenly the lights came on. Sitting in her leather armchair, the Queen of

Armenia was holding a small bottle in her hand, and she opened it carefully. With an attention to detail that could be noted even at a distance, she used a tiny brush to paint her fingernails. Then she stretched out her fingers, shaking them carefully so that the nail varnish would dry. Arthur was curious, impatiently wondering what she would do next. As if in response to this question, she drew herself up to her full height and began to dance. At first, she moved slowly, reaching out before her. It was as if a partner were in front of her, ready to take her into his arms. After a few minutes, she picked up the pace. Her black hair spun around, the shadow of her silhouette was thrown on the opposite wall. Halfway through a turn, she stumbled and stopped, her eyes fixed onto the floor. Arthur tried to see out what was happening and followed the woman's glance. A ball of fur was hunched up below her. It was a little grey cat. The Queen of Armenia picked it up and pressed it against her. But suddenly, in a violent and unexpected turn, she threw the animal at the nearest wall. The cat slid, turned, and writhed on the floor. It stopped moving. The Queen of Armenia came toward the window and Arthur was able to clearly make out her pale face behind the glass. Emotionless and statuesque, after a long pause, she put her hands to her face, craned her neck, and left the room. The white room was empty.

The next morning, Arthur felt exhausted, as if he had not slept. He was seized by a strong desire for coffee. As he put on the coffee pot, a note on the floor caught his eye. Someone must have slipped it under the door. He picked it up and read.

Dear Brian,

I can't believe you left without telling me or giving me your new address. You don't even have a cell phone, so it's impossible to get a hold of you. It looks like there is a new tenant in your apartment. I spoke to him by phone and asked him if he knew where you were. He claimed not to know you. I doubted it, but he wouldn't tell me anything. Brian, I'm your friend, and you mean a lot to me. I would like to see you, touch you, kiss you. What happened? Is there some big problem you can't tell me about? True, we've had our bad moments, but now things have changed. Last week, I didn't feel well, so I called Doctor Simon Leonoff. He saw me right away and we talked for a long time. I told him about something that happened to me in the subway when I was waiting for the train at the 96th Street station. The notice board said it was coming. A young guy with a beard, about thirty years old, came up to me, grabbed me by the arm, and tried to throw me onto the tracks. I screamed and pushed him away as hard as I could. A woman saw what was happening, but instead of helping me, she said, "Hey, Miss, calm down! What's going on?" What an idiot. She hadn't noticed anything. If you have a problem, there's no one you can count on to help. You're completely alone. When I turned around, the guy had disappeared (and now, you're the one who has disappeared… Let's not go there again). Luckily, Dr. Leonoff listened to my story. He even asked me to fill in some details. He asked me how I felt about the aggression on the platform. He wanted to know if I could fall asleep after that happened, and my reply was no, of course. Every night, I dream about the man with the beard, and he always says, "I'll get you next time." Leonoff gave me a prescription for some medicine I should take after dinner. He promised me: "Soon, you'll be doing better. You just have to be patient…" I have a follow-up appointment with him tomorrow. He's fantastic, and he always listens to me. Some people say that you can never find a doctor when you need one, but that's not true. Simon is always there when I need him.

Call me. Please. I'll be expecting you.
Yours, LM

Arthur was intrigued by this letter. He read it twice. He didn't know what to think, and decided to discuss it with his neighbor Linda Wells. When she opened the door, he offered to take her out to the restaurant nearby. She accepted, and a few minutes later, they were sitting at a table set with a vase of carnations.

"Do you know the guy that lived in my apartment before me?" he asked.

"Yes, vaguely. I would see him from time to time in the laundry room. Wait, what was his name…?"

"Brian."

"Ah, yes, that's right. Brian Fernández. He was from California. He played jazz on the clarinet. I think he worked in a music store. Sometimes I could hear him practicing through the wall. Nice guy, about thirty years old, brown hair pulled back in a pony tail. But one morning, I met him in the corridor and he told me he was leaving."

"Do you know where he is right now?"

"No, no idea. We didn't speak that much. He wasn't about to tell me his life story. You know, in New York people always come and go. It's like a merry-go-round. Everyone's detached, even disinterested: people don't mind being anonymous or alone. Why are you so interested in Brian?"

"Well, he disappeared into thin air, and I'm trying to help a lady who wants to find him.

Arthur told Linda about the phone call the night before and showed her the letter he'd found under his door. She read it, and sighed.

"That's wild. It looks like she's stalking him. Want some advice? Don't get involved! Love stories like this don't work out… it happens all the time."

"You're right, but I'm kind of intrigued. This woman seems really unhappy, and I would like to…"

"Arthur, you have a big heart," Linda joked. "What, so

you're like her personal private detective or something?"

"No, no, of course not. Another thing: I found a tie…"

"A tie?" Linda asked, confused. "What tie?"

"Brian left a nice silk tie in the closet."

"That's his goodbye present! Keep it. You can put it on next time you go out."

"Good idea. Want some dessert?

They ordered an apple pie with a big scoop of vanilla ice cream on top. Arthur pointed at the big building on the other side of the street.

"See the apartment on the tenth floor?" he asked.

"Yeah… and?"

"Well, I met the person who lives there."

"Oh yeah? You're already making friends in the neighborhood? You're fast! It usually takes a long time before people even say anything to each other around here."

"No, I didn't mean it that way," Arthur said, a bit annoyed. "It's just I keep seeing a woman behind the window."

"She's pretty, and you're spying on her? All you need is your Aston Martin."

"Look, instead of making fun of me, just try to guess who lives up there."

"In that nice building? Well, let's see. You need to be classy and rich to live there. I know… it must be one of Caroline Kennedy's cousins," Linda said, laughing.

"Wrong!" Arthur replied. "Any other ideas?"

"No, none. I don't read the tabloids. Go on, tell me. I give up."

"It's the Queen of Armenia."

"Who?"

"The Queen of Armenia. She emigrated to New York when her castle was destroyed. She moved into that apartment, just in front of our building."

"I didn't know that Armenia was a monarchy…"

"Well, no, it's hasn't been a monarchy for a long time. But this is my story, and I'm sticking to it. The monarchy has been reestablished!"

"You'll stop at nothing when you get obsessed!" she said.

Arthur put his hand on Linda's arm.

"Let me tell you the story of this Queen. She was living alone in her huge house after her husband left with a Persian prince to get rid of his country's invaders. She didn't hear about these two courageous soldiers for a long time, until one day a poor salt vendor knocked on the door to the palace. When she arrived, the man knelt before her, kissed her hands, and told her that the King had died valiantly in an ambush. The night after this tragic news, the entire region was destroyed by an earthquake. The tremors were so violent that they even shook Mount Ararat. But by some miracle, God did not completely abandon the Queen of Armenia. Under his protection, she managed to survive amidst the rubble. She dragged herself breathlessly through the engraved caskets that had caved in all around her and managed to escape. She walked for days through forests and villages in ruins. Massive trees had been felled by the quake and were lying on the ground. The birds were famished, and they crisscrossed the sky above her. When the hordes of barbarians saw this lonely figure in the countryside, they chased after her, with the intent to kill. She managed to get away, but she found herself on a path that got narrower and narrower. Eventually it disappeared in the brambles and thickets. Ahead there was a waterfall, so deep and strong that it would be impossible to cross. There was no way out. She was a prisoner. She fell asleep at the water's edge, exhausted, and certain that she was going to die. But the next night, when an aftershock hit, and the boulders high above plunged down into the gorge, the Queen was able to find a way to cross over to the other side and escape catastrophe."

"My storyteller from the East…"

As she said this, Linda smiled, happy to witness her friend's imagination in full throttle.

"You're taking off, Arthur!" she laughed. "Be careful, or you'll fly away."

He told Linda about the scene that had taken place in the apartment, and how he had seen the woman throw the cat against the wall.

"This Queen of yours is cruel. Sometimes, that's the price of survival, I guess. It would be better if you kept your distance."

Linda looked at Arthur, but he didn't say anything. She liked his blue eyes.

When night fell, Arthur went back to the lookout post behind his window. For the first time, the Queen of Armenia was no longer alone in her white room. A man with unkempt hair and a drained face was showing her some pictures that he hoisted one at a time against the wall before putting them down. It was too far for Arthur to see the pictures clearly, but he could make out abstract motifs that reminded him of Cubism in some pictures, while others echoed the Impressionist light of Renoir. The Queen of Armenia moved continually. She would go up to the canvas, step back, and then take a look at the paintings up close. She examined the works with a lively yet wary eye. Sometimes she passed her finger over the pictures as if to check that the paint was dry. After a long moment's hesitation, she picked out a canvas with no frame. The work was daubed with grey stripes of different hues, laid out carefully but dotted with haphazard spots of color here and there. Like an actress disappearing into the wings, the woman went into another room, and then came back carrying a small hammer in her right hand. The man rummaged in his pockets and took out a nail that he affixed to the wall. He hung up the picture and looked at the Queen of Armenia, waiting for her approval. As if in agreement, she nodded gently and dismissed the vendor. He picked up the other paintings, wrapped them in paper, and left.

Alone, the Queen of Armenia went to the other side of the room and examined the canvas. Arthur got the impression that she was moving her lips, talking to herself. He could not control his curiosity, however intrusive it felt to observe this woman, who was observing the painting she had just bought. Suddenly, to his great surprise, the Queen of Armenia leaned over a low table, not quite visible from his vantage point. She picked up a glass. And then everything started to move quickly. With a flick of her wrist, she dashed its entire contents against the picture on the wall. The grey paint dissolved immediately, and produced slimy streaks on the canvas, lit by splashes of color. The liquid ran down the wall and formed a puddle on the floor. The work had become an indistinct, thick, dirty mess. The Queen of Armenia smiled slightly, as if she was satisfied at having destroyed her recent purchase. She turned off the light, and darkness enveloped the room.

Arthur was deeply disturbed by what he had just witnessed. Uninvited, as a midnight spy, he had broken into a universe of madness, and witnessed a dark intimacy unfold on the other side of the street. His own behavior surprised him. Why was he playing this game? Why was he so fascinated with the woman in the purple dress? And why had he made her out to be the Queen of Armenia? After all, the bond between his sister and her Ottoman fiancé, a relationship that he could neither support nor condemn at the time, had driven him away from both his family and his roots. Could that be the very reason for his attraction? Was he going to continue with this fantasy, telling Linda about the painting with the grey lines, picked out so carefully, and then ruined a few seconds later? There was no doubt in his mind that she would be an eager audience, smiling, lips pursed, ready to be carried off by his imagination.

Arthur took down the book by Elvira Clusky and read two chapters of *The Arsonist*, wanting to take his mind off things. The book was full of surprising developments. In the Brooklyn neighborhood where the author had set the story, the fires kept raging with no apparent logic or provocation. The criminal's first target were industrial warehouses, fortunately unoccupied as the explosions went off. Then came the stores, fortunately not during opening hours. In spite of close investigations and heightened security, the suspect remained at large. The tension mounted when, a month later, the arsonist set fire to an elementary school just as the children were going to school. The principal risked his life to evacuate the students. Incensed and worried out of their minds, the parents organized themselves to take turns guarding the school. They accused the police of incompetence, even complicity, as one particularly aggressive father suggested. Absorbed in the rhythm of the novel and swept away by its forceful plot, Arthur was startled when he suddenly heard loud knocking. Somebody was beating furiously against the door. Irritated by the interruption, Arthur stood up, book in hand. He went to the door, and demanded who was calling so unexpectedly. He couldn't make out the response. It was barely audible. The banging stopped, so he repeated the question. The corridor fell silent, and then a woman's voice called: "Brian, are you there?"

"You again?" Arthur began to shout angrily. "I already told you that Brian doesn't live here anymore. There's nothing here for you. Please leave!"

The visitor did not reply. For a moment, Arthur thought that he had convinced her to leave. He was about to start reading again, when he heard,

"Help me, I'm begging you. Help me…"

The voice was sad, pleading. Arthur's voice softened.

"Sorry, but there's nothing I can do for you. The best thing is to forget Brian. Leave this building, go back home."

"I have no home, the woman said. I'm alone. Open the door, I beg you."

Was it pity? Was it curiosity? Or was it a mixture of both? Arthur opened the door, and there on the doorstep was the Queen of Armenia in her purple dress. She was haggard and disheveled, shivering. He motioned for her to pass. "Come on in. I was waiting for you." She did not move. He stepped back to let her in, but it was too late. When he looked up, the woman had disappeared. She seemed to have flown away.

Following this visit, Arthur was overcome by malaise. How silly of him to have turned this solitary and unbalanced figure into the Queen of Armenia, fleeing brutality and natural disasters. He knew that all stories of exodus, real or imaginary, ended up drawing you into a single narrative. You are never safe, even in another country, another house, another era. The attackers have no problem traversing years, generations. They will seek you out, a dagger in their hands, and slit your throat.

It was now Arthur who wished to flee, to turn the page and slip into an existence free of stress. He called Linda and suggested they spend the evening at a bar on the Hudson, only accessible via a path leading toward the grey waters of the river. When they met up an hour later, sitting at a wrought iron table against the parapet, they burst out laughing. Without planning it, they were both dressed up. Linda had put on her yellow shoes and Arthur had put on the blue tie from his closet.

VI

When Characters Change Their Names

A blue spot shimmered in the darkness, lighting up the screen. Eric Landolt was sitting at the computer, listening carefully to make sure that his colleagues had finally left the office. Yes, he was alone in the muffled rooms of the bank. No one who happened to discover him would be surprised by his presence this late, since everyone knew that he often stayed after hours. In fact, they often gossiped about it at the coffee machine. "Have you noticed how obsessed Landolt gets with work? He thinks he's Stakhanov. What he wants is his end-of-year bonus, and he'll get it, for sure. I bet he doesn't see his wife very often. And he must see his son even less…" The evening before, as they left a meeting, Luc Verdier, a mustachioed man who was more insolent (or perhaps franker) than most, brought it up directly. Eric took offense and snapped back, as if he had been stung. Addressing himself to nobody in particular, he replied, "I have a knack for dealing with fiscal matters better than anyone else. I'm the lawyer you choose if you don't want to screw things up. You know that, right? So leave me alone." Eric Landolt could easily envisage his growing reputation in the world of business and international law and was proud of his prospects. After all, his colleagues' jealousy simply proved that he was the best. He began at the bottom of the ladder when he first graduated, and in just a few years, had become the boss's protégé.

Cautiously, Eric entered an access code on a website, and *Venus in the Garden* loaded up after a few seconds. A smiling statue appeared on the home page, her head crowned with hibiscus roses. A stylized map appeared and invited the user first to choose a continent, then a city. In just a few clicks, Eric landed in New York, and located the pictures that he had identified the previous evening. He examined a series of young women with attractive faces – and bodies. Among the beautiful pictures, he noticed twenty-eight-year-old Luna. He decided to write to her before she disappeared off the screen, just as mysteriously as she had materialized. Luna was smiling, as if she enjoyed the attention. He hadn't dared contact her until now, but this evening he felt so alone. He wanted to be in someone's presence, it didn't matter who. He oscillated between embarrassment and curiosity, but was slowly drawn into this electronic journey. Using his credit card, he paid the entrance fee to the site, and space and time no longer mattered. A generic message loaded on the screen: "Welcome to our platform! With *Venus in the Garden*, you can now meet women from all over the world. They'll be eager to give you their undivided attention! Make all the acquaintances you've dreamed of, from Oslo to Tokyo. Come on in, our doors are open!" The fine print explained the conditions under which users could, in the language of the website, contact three "correspondents." If he didn't find what he was looking for, he could pay a further fee for more options.

As soon as he selected his companion, it was as if Eric had turned into his younger self on the night before a first date. He was no longer the arrogant lawyer, overachieving and disliked among his peers, ready to win over clients with high-level legal advice. He was taken back to his timid adolescence, and didn't dare touch the keyboard. He drafted some words on a slip of yellow paper next to the computer, wanting to roll up his shirt sleeves, create a new identity for himself, and start a different life. He stared at the screen, convincing himself that imagination could enhance or even transform reality. He was the actor in the wings, leaning over a mirror in the dressing room, putting on his makeup before going on stage. He wrote:

Dear Luna,

I'm thirty-two years old, and I live in Europe. I'm not going to tell you my life story, but here are some details. Last year, I lost my wife in a car accident in Italy, near Venice. It was a terrible shock when she died. It's hard for me to get over her loss, but I'd like to turn the page, even if it is difficult. I don't have any children.

"How melodramatic," he thought. "The widower whose life has been torn apart, and who now needs a nice girl to console him. No, that's too typical. I should try something else. Act interested in her, rather than talking about myself."

Luna, what a pretty name! It must be a pseudonym that you've invented, as I imagine everyone does on this site. I wonder where you're from. Maybe a Nordic country? For some reason I can't explain, I can hear you speaking Swedish… It has to be because of the photo that I can see on the screen. Or maybe you were born in New York, and your parents are immigrants who went to the States before you were born. They baptized you Ingrid. You haven't returned to your homeland yet, but you intend to go next year.

He re-read both texts and then tore the paper up into tiny pieces. Standing, he went to the library and got a beer out of a cooler concealed inside a drawer. That would give him some inspiration, he thought. Suddenly, he heard a noise from the corridor. It was Carmen, a cleaner in a white apron. She had come into the office without knocking. Eric abruptly turned off the screen, which still bore Luna's frozen smile. He gave Carmen the ritual "Hello, how are you?" and watched her distractedly empty the trash and dust the furniture. Now she was leaving, along with her smell of bleach, pushing the cart of cleaning products before her. Eric cracked open the beer and after thinking a moment, decided to write a very quick note and send it immediately, before he had time to think about it or add anything else.

Luna,
We could write to each other, talk, or see each other—your choice! What do you think? All my best. Paul Lamar.

He was pleased with this nice-sounding pseudonym: Paul Lamar. He wondered if he'd get a reply. What if the site was a trap, or, worse, a swindle that would compromise the details of his credit card? And if pretty Luna did not exist? Was she just bait to lure unsuspecting lonely men? And what if Anne found out that after telling her that he had a very important deadline to meet, he had actually stayed in the office late into the evening on a dating site under a false name? Would she be taken aback, scornful, or worried? Would she pummel him with questions, or would she just give him the dirty look that she often used these days? Eric did not want to envisage his wife's reaction. He would rather just pay the fee and enter the imaginary world, *Venus in the Garden.*

After the wedding, Anne and Eric had slowly grown further and further apart. There was no open conflict, but you could sense a gradual distancing, like two tracks that were originally parallel, diverging from each other little by little. On the face of it, everything was fine for each of them. They looked like the perfect couple. A house on the lake (thanks to the generosity of their parents), both with an enviable professional career, a lively spirit, strong and youthful bodies, and above all, four years ago, the arrival of a son. Joseph's birth had brought them great happiness, but no intimacy. On the contrary: they had different ideas about his upbringing. It was true that they worried about their son's behavior, which was sometimes peculiar. He was a secretive child, with a keen intelligence, but he seemed to hide in a world only he knew. But they never managed to really speak of it. In fact, both of them would avoid the topic. Eric didn't think that they should give in to their son's whims (he often said: "that kid is winding us around his little finger"); Anne could not understand her son's reactions, so she sought refuge in her work. They would often get back late at night and after Joseph was asleep, share a light meal and idle conversation. "Did you have a good day? Did you see what they're doing on the bridge?" etc. After slipping into something more comfortable, they would sit silently in the living room and watch TV or read for a while. They would eventually go to their shared bed, each alone.

Suddenly, the screen flickered. Eric was surprised at how quickly the response had arrived. He took off his tie and threw it on a nearby chair. The text appeared:

Dear Paul,

Thank you for writing me. I honestly didn't expect to get a reply. People exchange so many messages on this website. I was certain that nobody would notice me. I'm happy that I was wrong.

For the time being, we can send messages so that we can get to know one another better. Maybe someday we can meet up, perhaps halfway between Europe and America. What do you think about the Azores?

What can I tell you about myself? I was born in Buffalo and I grew up on Lake Erie, near the border with Canada. The weather is harsh up there. The winter is never-ending, which is why I left two years ago. My parents didn't really want me to go. They thought I was too young to live alone in a big city. But I was ready! I asked Scott Thompson, a childhood friend, to rent a truck and help me move some furniture out of my room. (Not many things, actually: my bed, a padded red armchair and a small desk that I love, which my grandmother gave me on my fifteenth birthday.) I found a job in New York in a health food store, Fillmore and Cie. They export their goods all over the world, and the business is getting bigger every year. It's a good job even though my boss is constantly insulting me. She's like the Big Bad Wolf or something! In the evening, I always have to show her what I've done that day, and if she manages to find a mistake, she makes me fix it before I can leave. I would love to escape and go back to my apartment on West 93rd Street. It's tiny, and the walls are bare, but I love it there. While I save up to buy some pictures, I could hang up a poster, maybe of the Caribbean, which I'm obsessed with. I'm happy because I've finally found my own path.

Well, I don't want to bother you with all my stories. I'll tell you more later. It's your turn now. I'd like to know more about you.

Luna

P.S. You're right: Luna is not my real name. I made it up, but you know what? I think it's pretty!

Eric Landolt, the prominent lawyer, was instantly carried away by the charm of this simple letter, this natural introduction ("If Luc Verdier could see me in front of Venus and her hibiscus, he would die laughing…") Eric had made a virtual friend, of course, but one who was an escape from his familiar language and world, and above all from his wife, whose seriousness, determination, and "good girl" demeanor now bothered him. He replied immediately.

Luna,

I read your letter, and would love to know more about you. What's a pretty girl like you doing posting your photo on a website? I'm sure you have tons of opportunities to meet people your own age in New York, don't you?

My best wishes, or, if I can be so bold, a hug and a kiss.
P.

You're right, Paul, I do have a lot of opportunities. Not only that, but Scott Thompson often sends me messages telling me that he wants to come to New York and take me out. But so far, I haven't accepted. I like him a lot. When we were sixteen and lived on the same street in Buffalo, we even used to be on kissing terms. It's simple. I don't want a lover (at least not right now). You want to know why? It'll shock you, but it's because of my shoes. Yes, you read that right. I bought some high-heeled shoes in Bloomingdale's, and they cost me a fortune. My boss doesn't think they are appropriate for the office. She says that they were made for a ball or a gala, not for work. She keeps telling me that I have to respect Fillmore and Cie's dress code: you're not allowed to dress provocatively! A few weeks ago, I went to the movies with a Spanish student, Enrique. Afterwards, he invited me back to his place for a glass of wine. We drank one bottle, and then another. I was already starting not to see straight when Enrique asked me to take off my shoes. He said he loved them and wanted to touch the leather. I didn't resist. I took them off. As soon as I was barefoot, Enrique put his hand on my knee, stroked my leg and then put his hand up my skirt. It was dark in the room and I was scared. I tried to put the light on, but he wouldn't let me. When I asked him to leave, he wouldn't listen. I pushed him away and got up. He started to shout that I was a flirt, and a tease, and I had to get out or else things would get nasty. Once I got out on the street, it started raining. I ran back home.

So now you see, Paul, why I hide behind my computer. But I'm happy to meet you. Write to me, OK? I'd be very interested to hear back from you.

Venus in the Garden afforded Luna the anonymity to pour out her feelings, and this pleased Eric. "This girl, on the other side of the ocean, is so naïve, it's almost touching. I will never meet her. I can tell her my true story with no fear. It's not worth making things up. I've got no reason to lie to her. The actor can take off his mask."

My dear Luna,

That guy Enrique is a jerk. You're lucky you got away from him. You should have been more careful, but that's no excuse. I hope you can put this episode behind you soon. I wonder if you still wear those shoes… they don't seem to be bringing you much luck, even if they are from Bloomingdale's.

I'm not sure if my life will be of much interest to you. To make a long story short, my marriage is in crisis. My wife and I care about each other, though. She's beautiful and intelligent. When I met her, she was the doctor on duty in the emergency room. I'd had an accident on my bike, and the ambulance took me there. I fell for her lively attitude and her beautiful dark hair. After I was discharged, I managed to invite her for coffee, and that was the beginning of our relationship. Her name is Anne (I don't mind telling you that); between her parents, her brother Arthur and her aunt Becca, they're a real clan. They have their problems, of course, but they always manage to get over them. They're the kind of people that pull together like a rugby team when they have to. At first, they accepted me with open arms. I was almost like the Messiah. Every Sunday, they invited me to a great meal, followed by expensive cognac. It was fantastic. But later on, I found out why. When I was alone with Becca one day, she told me that just before Anne met me, she was about to marry a Turk. For that family, the relationship was out of the question. There was such a big scandal that the wedding never took place. As Becca said, laughing, the Ottoman engagement was over.

I like those people and I love my wife, but now I understand that for her, I was more of a replacement than a real husband (well, I fit the bill, although she would never have described me that way). Today, our lives, our circumstances (you can use whatever word you please) are pulling us apart, and I wonder whether sooner or later, we are going to leave one another for good.

Suddenly, Eric Landolt stopped writing. He was surprised at how easily he had begun to confide in Luna. For the first time, he was able to articulate what had happened with Mehmet, and realized that he had never actually taken his place. He was the backup, the reserve, the understudy that takes on the role of main actor when needed. Normally so proud of himself, Eric was shaken by a truth that he had not fully understood until that point. He had been living with his head in the sand.

I'm mostly unhappy because of Joseph, our son. He's a difficult kid to understand because he lives in his own world. He likes to hide in the house. When you get back home from work in the evening, he won't come down and see you until you call him for a long time. Perhaps that's his way of avoiding the stress. He must sense something even though we try never to fight in front of him. Joseph is really close to a young Brazilian woman who we've paid to take care of him since he was born. He spends so much time with her that he's starting to speak Portuguese!

This electronic correspondence lasted for several weeks. In the evenings, Eric would wait impatiently for his colleagues to leave so that he could log on to *Venus in the Garden*. He was always excited for their virtual encounters, and when she didn't show up, it would drive him to despair. Then, unexpectedly, a last message arrived.

Paul,

I've been lying to you. Enrique doesn't exist: I invented him to make myself sound more interesting. My life is actually much simpler. I don't have a lot to tell you, but even though I have never seen you, I feel close to you. Your sincerity has touched me and I can't keep playing the part of a victim who has had a bad experience. Anyway, I don't think we should write to each other anymore.

I wonder what will happen to you now. I understand that you are going through a rough patch. Perhaps you'll separate from your wife, but you'll never leave your son. It sounds like your bond with him is unbreakable.

Thinking of you,

Luna

P.S. My yellow shoes actually do exist! Oh, and one more thing. My real name is Linda.

Anne couldn't settle down. As she got to the coffee shop, she was beset by a swirl of emotions. Of course, she wanted to see Mehmet again, to know what had become of him, and if he had changed at all. She asked herself what she was doing by agreeing to meet up with him again. Was it really a good idea to revisit the past, and risk reopening this wound that had taken so long to heal? Would she want to tell him about her tumultuous relationship with Eric or describe the worries that she had for her son? She hesitated, torn between desire and fear.

A few days earlier, when she got Mehmet's message telling her that he was going to be in Geneva, she was tempted not to reply, to delete the message. All she had to do was swipe her finger across the screen, and just like that, she could tell herself that it had all been a dream, that her Ottoman fiancé had not appeared: he belonged forever to the past. But curiosity won the day, and she arranged to see him at the *café des Ormes*, near the medical faculty where they used to meet up after class. Perhaps, she now told herself, it would have been better to go somewhere different. A more neutral environment would have been free from the burdens of the past.

Anne went into the bistro and glanced around. Mehmet wasn't there. She sat in a dark corner, where she could see people come and go but not be seen herself. When the waiter came to take her order, she told him, "I'm expecting a friend. He should be here soon." The waiter shrugged and left. She smiled to herself, amused: "I'm expecting a friend…" What if he didn't come? What if he missed his plane, or got lost on the way? Perhaps involuntarily, she had chosen the easiest thing to say: "He should be here soon." After all, even though Mehmet had taken the initiative to write to her, perhaps he had the same doubts as her. Maybe he wouldn't show up. But then, wouldn't he let her know? She wasn't sure.

To save face, she picked up a paper from the adjoining table and tried in vain to read an article with the gloomy title, "Europe Adrift." Her thoughts wandered. Nothing made any sense. She couldn't string the words together logically. The text was illustrated by an incomprehensible graph depicting two colored lines that intersected and then separated again. She put the paper down. The waiter was behind a line of bottles. He pushed a button, and a playlist came on.

Anne looked up and saw a slender young man dressed in a black waistcoat striding into the café. She smiled and motioned toward him, but he did not react. At first, she was puzzled, but then looked more carefully and realized she'd made a mistake. "Now I've hit rock bottom," she thought. "I must be in a really bad way… I thought it was Mehmet. Of all the times I've put my foot in it, this takes the cake. They don't even look alike!" She pushed her chair back against the wall, trying to disappear. The man came over and asked, "Do we know each other?" She hesitated before replying casually: "Sorry! I'm very shortsighted and I get people mixed up. I'm waiting for someone else."

The young man took a pair of glasses out of his pocket and waved them in his right hand. "Well, if you ever need it, I know a good eye doctor…" He winked and left. A figure appeared behind him. It was Mehmet, quizzical and insecure. When he saw Anne, he held out both hands toward her.

"Anoush, it's you…"

"Yes, yes, but please don't call me Anoush anymore."

"What?"

"My name's Anne now. Sit down. Let me tell you all about it!"

They looked at each other in silence. Both were overcome by feelings that they tried to disguise. They exchanged some small talk instead.

"Did you have a good trip?" Anne asked.

"Yes, the plane was half empty. It was a pretty uneventful flight."

"Are you going to be here for a few days?"

"Until Sunday. Then I'm going to meet up with my cousin in Paris."

Mehmet pointed at the photos on the wall.

"The décor is still the same. I recognize the pictures of the Alps and the parachutists in mid-air."

"Remember? We used to come in this café on Monday evenings after cardiology class. We'd share our notes…"

"And we'd look at the diagrams in the book," he added. "We even studied for an exam at this table. Tell me, when was the last time we saw one another? I can't quite remember…"

"Five years ago. Just before you left for Turkey. You haven't changed a bit, and yet I just mixed you up with someone else!"

"Oh yes? You didn't recognize me? I can assure you, that could never happen to me because you're always on my mind. Sometimes I even see women in Istanbul who remind me of you. Tell me about your life."

"Well, it's a lot to explain in just a couple of minutes. After I graduated, I worked in a clinic for a while. That's where I met my husband. He was my patient."

Mehmet interrupted her.

"You got married? You married an Armenian? I would have bet on that. I imagine your parents must be so relieved. It's all they ever wanted. There was no way they would have gone along with your 'Ottoman engagement.' That's an expression I'll never forget…"

A harsher tone crept into Mehmet's voice.

"Let's not go through all that again," Anne said. "But if you really do want to know, no, I didn't marry an Armenian. Are you happy now? I have a little son, called Joseph. He loves music. What about you? Are you married?"

"No. I was in a relationship with the same woman for a long time. We even lived together, but we broke up last year. I don't really know why. It had kind of run its course, that's all."

"More drama then?" Anne asked.

"No, and no bad feelings. Now I'm a free man. You're right, we shouldn't dwell on the past, but you have to admit, your parents… How do you say this in French? They really screwed things up."

"What? What are you talking about?"

"I'm just saying I still think it was their fault we broke up. They would never have accepted our marriage. Never."

"Don't exaggerate, Mehmet."

He reminded her that his name alone had turned him into a perverse killer in their eyes. As far as the Simonian family was concerned, he was a blood-stained criminal who, to put it bluntly, was responsible for the genocide. He added, "And you let them tell you what to do. You didn't defend me."

"That's not true. Anyway, you don't understand. I was torn between you and my roots. I was stuck in the middle."

Anne's eyes misted over. She remembered how she felt at the family gathering that April 24th, when she had announced her plans to marry Mehmet. She could still hear her father's voice, his indignation and reproaches. How defeated she had felt.

The waiter arrived and took their order.

"The genocide was a hundred years ago," Mehmet said, "but you would think it was yesterday. It won't let go of us."

"I think you know why."

"Tell me…"

"When you deny facts, and refuse to own up to them, they don't just go away. It's the opposite. You bring them back to life. They killed an entire population and now they want to smother it a second time, with silence. It's impossible. The evidence proves what happened. People need courage to face it, accept it, and tell the truth. Only then will there be peace. Maybe."

Anne did not dare tell her ex-fiancé that sometimes, at night, she would lie there powerlessly, listening to the screams of the dead. They wanted reparations, demanding justice and asking the living to act in their stead. She added:

"See, it's like a weight, and it follows me around. I wanted to let it go, so I gave up the name Anoush. My name is Anne now. Do you understand?"

"I do understand that the world is divided in two groups: the victims and the persecutors, those who died and those who killed."

"Don't act like you're surprised by that. These are the lessons of history."

"And what if history has confused the issue?"

"Confused the issue?" Anne was beginning to get annoyed. "What do you mean? You're mixing it all up. Explain yourself!"

Mehmet looked at Anne and paused. Then, lowering his voice, he said, "Last year, I discovered something by accident. You'll never guess."

"Are you going to give me a clue?"

"Don't even try. I'm going to tell you, but get ready for a shock. Anoush, I have Armenian blood, too!"

Anne looked at him in astonishment.

"What on earth are you talking about? Have you gone crazy?"

"Listen to me. My grandmother, my father's mother, was Armenian."

"And you didn't know?"

"No, nobody did. She hid her identity her entire life: her identity and her story. But she didn't want to take her secret to the grave, so she waited for a moment when we could be alone together to tell me the truth. When she was a child, she lived with her parents and younger brother in a village near Adana, in the south of Turkey. Her father was a miller, and she grew up in a mill. One evening, as the sun went down, she heard a loud noise over the wheat fields. She looked through a crack in the wall. At first, she couldn't see anything, then soldiers suddenly appeared on horseback behind the apricot trees. She heard the horses neighing through the mist, and they moved so quickly that big clouds of dust blew up all around them. Once they got to the door of the mill the soldier jumped off and ran inside. The youngest one was only about eighteen. He didn't even have a beard. He ran up to the miller and thrust a knife into his throat, leaving my grandmother to witness her father die in a pool of blood. Her mother began to scream and tried to protect her newborn. She stood in front of the crib, but she was pushed outside and the baby was thrown to the ground. My grandmother managed to hide behind a dresser lined with jars of homemade jam. Terrified of the attackers, she threw up in her skirt. They were shouting and ransacked the house. When they left, she didn't move for hours, sure that they would come back to kill her. The next day, at daybreak, she left her hiding place and found the bodies of her father and the baby. There was no trace of her mother… she never saw her again."

Mehmet stopped. His throat was parched. Anne, on the verge of tears, could barely bring herself to speak. She looked at him inquisitively. He carried on.

"Next door there was a small farm where an Ottoman family lived. When the farmer saw the child coming out of the mill all alone, he guessed what had happened, so he took the little girl by the hand and led her home. There were no questions or explanations. A few days later, he told her that her name would now be Deniz and that she was going to live with him and his family. He asked her never to tell anyone about what she had been through and to forget her old name, Vartouhi. From there on out, my grandmother never cried again. It was as if her tears had dried up forever. When things were too much to bear, she would go outside, to where the donkey was tied up in its stall. The donkey would recognize her, and shake its head when she arrived. She would hug it and stroke its muzzle. One day, local employees arrived with industrial machinery and in a few hours, they had torn down the mill. She realized that she had lost almost everything, except the trees and the juicy yellow apricots she would pick when they were in season. This was all my grandmother remembered of her childhood. She left the farm at the age of eighteen. In town, she met my grandfather and married him without revealing anything about her past. She never told him her real name or her real religion, so he never found out the truth. Now it is too late: he died last spring. I'm the first one to learn her secret."

Anne was shaken to the core by Mehmet's story. She wondered how this child had survived her family's loss and managed to take on a new identity. All her life, she had locked the truth in a profound silence, and thrown away the key.

Anne put her hands around Mehmet's, sending an electric shock between them. For a moment, she could not resist imagining a different end to their story. What would have happened had she uncovered the truth earlier? Would the barrier between them have been lifted? How would Aram have reacted, had he known that the Ottoman fiancé, the one he so violently rejected, had inherited such a fragile and fractured past? But Anne had to tell herself that there was no way back, not a chance. She began to dream that she was walking beside Mehmet on a narrow path bordering the banks of Lake Geneva. They were holding hands with their child. They stopped under a tree and Mehmet picked up some flat stones and threw them into the lake. That was the spot where Anne would observe and envy the deft, accurate way he was able to skim stones. For no particular reason, her mind took her back to that moment in the past. She followed the concentric circles as they surfaced in the water. The ripples got bigger and bigger, and then disappeared. Darkness came over the horizon, so Mehmet picked up the child and put it on his shoulders. Then the image fell away, and the décor of the *café des Ormes* came back into view. "We should go back," he said. "It's getting dark." Throngs of students poured out of the university toward the bar, beers in their hands. They were laughing and talking in loud voices. "That's what we used to do," Anne remembered. She leaned toward Mehmet.

"My Ottoman fiancé… she said, affectionately. All of a sudden, you're part Armenian. Now we've seen everything!"

"Yes," he answered. "Pity it's too late."

Intermission

Armenia, my legacy. The melody of your name, which runs sweet and insistent through my blood, is a mixture of marvel and misfortune.

Armenia, my legacy. An incandescent treasure whose flames both burn and pacify me, radiate throughout my being, and then disappear.

Armenia, my legacy. The battleground where I will conquer my rage, the boat of my exile that I must steer towards calmer waters in the port.

Armenia, my legacy. The tale of my family, which has been bestowed on me as a talisman. With this talisman, I will write a book.

Harry Koumrouyan

PART TWO

Joseph's Story

VII

The Disappearance of Madame Butterfly

Joseph liked to hide. He had his favorite places - behind the red silk curtains in the living room and under the low table in the foyer. The table was covered with a damask tablecloth that fell over the sides, forming a screen. When Lolo was looking for him, she would call out his name in a loud voice, but he didn't always reply. She would pretend to be angry, warning him, "Joseph, I'm going to get mad!" But after a few minutes' silence, she would lower her voice. "I made you some rice pudding, but if you don't come out, I'm going to have to eat it all by myself." The strategy often worked. Joseph came out of his hiding place like a genie from a bottle, sprinting toward the kitchen. Lolo, the young woman who had taken care of him since he was born, would wait for him with a smile, holding a bowl in her hand. He would grab the spoon and gulp down the rice, the wet grains running down his chin. Lolo watched him eat and said gently, "My little lad, people would think you were starving to death…"

Four years earlier, Joseph's parents had hired Lolo to take care of their son because they themselves didn't have a lot of time on their hands. Anne Landolt was a doctor for an international organization. Eric worked until all hours in one of Geneva's best-known private banks. It had diligently served the entitled Protestant class since the early nineteenth century. Anne and Eric treated Lolo with courtesy, but still kept a respectable distance, addressing her in a formal way. But they always made sure to give her a generous gift at Christmas. Anne had even presented her with a pink cashmere sweater that she didn't wear. When Lolo heard Joseph's parents refer to her as "the maid," she was

119

surprised. She didn't know the word, but she remembered it and looked it up in her pocket dictionary. After that, she would think to herself, "I'm their son's maid."

Lolo was an attentive and observant presence in the household. One morning, as she was hanging up Eric's suit, a letter fell out from the inside pocket, so she picked it up and glanced at it. The senior associate of the bank had congratulated Eric on his professional performance and told him that he would be receiving a raise, by what Lolo considered to be quite a large sum of money. She opened the closet and put the suit away. She was supposed to fold Anne's blouses, too, so she went into the bedroom, not pausing to knock, because she thought she was alone. But unlike most days, Anne had not gone to work. She was lying on the bed, and her eyes were puffy, as though she had been crying. Lolo muttered an excuse and left the room, unnoticed.

She had learned to spot trouble. Her presence in Switzerland was illegal because she had no work permit. She had also never told Joseph's parents her real story. They did not understand the circumstances surrounding her departure from Rio. She had entered the country on a tourist visa, certain now that she had surmounted the final hurdle and made it to the promised land. Anne and Eric did not pry or press her for details about her past, and she preferred it that way. When she saw groups of police officers at the station, she always worried that they would ask her for her papers. The only person who ever asked her about her life in Rio, however, was Luis, the Colombian gardener who came by the Landolt house once a week. "Are you married?" he asked, without a hint of discretion. She shook her finger. "Ah, it can't be true! A pretty girl like you…"

Lolo began work early. When she arrived at the house, which had been built on a hill overlooking Lake Geneva, everything was calm and dark. Lolo opened the kitchen door and could smell the white lilacs, so close to the wall that she could almost touch them. She wore a cotton apron and a blue skirt. Anne had asked her not to wear pants, with a curt "That wouldn't be appropriate."

In the morning, Eric would leave for work so early that Lolo never saw him go. At nine, Anne would appear alone in the kitchen, often dressed in dark clothing that accentuated her thin frame. She would stand against the table holding a china cup, drinking coffee that Lolo had prepared for her. Then there were the day's instructions. "Take Joseph out for a walk. It will do him good to get some air… and don't forget his hat." Lolo never said it, but she always thought that the boy would prefer to play in his room than take a walk in the woods. Either way, she would find a way to convince him to get out of the house, though. She would transform the trees and the flowers into living creatures and pretend that a sorcerer had given them magical powers. She was sure that the boy's imagination would take over from there.

"I'll be back late tonight," Anne said. "And so will Eric. He's going to a hockey match with his friends. I hope that's alright with you."

"No problem. I'll wait for you."

Lolo was happy to stay with Joseph. She was very attached to him. "The little boy I take care of could be my own son," she would write to her mother in Rio. When Joseph woke up and came down to the kitchen, Anne would give him a tender but awkward hug. "She acts scared that he's going to crease her coat, or spill something on it," Lolo thought. When Anne got ready to leave and kissed her son, his reactions were impossible to predict. Sometimes he was indifferent. Other times, he became so angry that she couldn't calm him down. Powerless, she would leave Lolo to pick up the pieces, barely able to hide her embarrassment and disappointment. Lolo would sing him one of her mother's Brazilian lullabies. She could remember each and every word. Little by little, the boy would calm down.

But Joseph worried Lolo. He was a loner, by turns shy or aggressive toward other children. The young woman was particularly perturbed by the game of hide and seek that he loved to play. He would disappear into the most unexpected of places, staying put for a good long time unless Lolo went to find him. She was always able to discover his hiding places, but when his parents returned home in the evening, Joseph would never appear. It was as if he didn't expect them to come back and had forgotten that they even existed.

One Saturday evening, Anne and Eric invited their neighbors over for a drink. Carla and Aldo Monte were an older couple, former opera singers, and Lolo liked them a lot. When they got to the house, they called Joseph down to say hello, but he just went and hid. The hosts tried to disguise their embarrassment, engaging in small talk about the weather and a recent hail storm, which "in mere seconds, can you believe it…" had destroyed some of the local vineyards. Once they had moved on from the weather, Eric mumbled under his breath, "I wonder what has happened to that boy." Carla had brought up four children, and decided to summon Joseph in her own way. She got up from the chair, glanced at her husband, and started to sing a Puccini aria. Her voice may not have been as strong as it once was, but it reverberated throughout the house and even into the garden. Anne and Eric were surprised, and even more so when Joseph suddenly appeared from behind the lilac bushes, curious as to what was going on. He went into the hall and took Lolo's hand. "My wife sings great, don't you think?" Aldo Monte asked, looking at him. "We're so happy to see you!" Lolo was relieved to have found the boy. She wondered if the singer was going to continue with her magical song, but she didn't dare ask.

Carla sipped on her drink and laughed. "Master Puccini! A great composer…" She continued, paying special attention to Joseph, "It's a very sad story, Madame Butterfly. Her real name was Cio Cio San and she lived in Japan." Joseph listened attentively, and wanted her to finish the story. Eric interrupted his son, telling him that it was time to go to bed. Joseph didn't move.

"I'll tell you the story of Madame Butterfly the next time I come over to visit," Carla said.

"It's getting late." Eric was now raising his voice. "Go to bed. I don't want to have to tell you again."

Lolo placed her hand on the child's shoulder, and they left the room without saying a word.

Upstairs in his room, Joseph asked Lolo if she knew the story of Madame Butterfly. She said she didn't, but reminded him of Carla's promise. "You'll find out what happens very soon. In the meantime, you can make something up. What do you think happened to Madame Butterfly?" The boy was lost in thought for a while. "I think she left her family and went off somewhere," he decided. Lolo drew the curtains and wished him good night.

Back in the kitchen, she cleared the sink and swept the floor. Anne and Eric were on the balcony having another drink with their guests. Lolo could hear their conversation through the open window.

"I worry about Joseph," Anne said. "He's so peculiar, so different from other children his age. When the neighbors' kids come over, he lets them borrow his toys, but then he pays them no mind. He'll disappear, or go off looking for Lolo. Soon he'll be speaking Portuguese …"

Lolo wondered what to make of that remark. Anne continued, this time to Carla.

"You sing beautifully, it's true, but I would never have thought that a small child like him could get so interested in opera."

"Easy! Your son loves music. The only reason his reaction seems strange to you is that you can't imagine such a thing."

"Well, of course I can imagine it. I'm his mother! It just surprises me, that's all."

Carla tried to reassure her.

"Don't worry. You know, sometimes we have a hard time understanding the people that are closest to us, even our children. No matter how hard we try, we love them without actually understanding them."

Aldo Monte looked at his wife, and then repeated, laughing,

"Exactly. No matter how hard we try, we don't always understand them!"

"What made you sing that song?" Eric asked, slightly irritated.

"It's the art of surprise …"

"Surprise? What do you mean?"

"Joseph is used to hearing his name and not answering. So I thought it would be good to do something different, to reel him in …"

From a dark corner of the kitchen, Lolo heard the conversation. Her instinct told her that Carla was right. Lolo didn't know anything about opera, but she could draw a clear link between Puccini's aria and the Brazilian lullabies.

"And just like that, a musical composer turns into a child psychologist," Eric said, ironically. "Personally, I think that the child has a problem and needs a firm hand. Maybe even a change of scenery."

This scared Lolo. Were they going to move? To separate her from Joseph?

The trees cast a dark shadow over the garden. Soon, the singers rose, thanked their hosts and said their goodbyes in Italian.

It rained heavily the next day, with violent gusts of wind. Toward midday, Lolo called for Joseph to come and eat, but he didn't reply. She called again, but the house was silent. Lolo went into his room and found it empty. She began to look in all his hiding places, but couldn't find him anywhere. She went down to the cellar and the laundry room: in vain. She called his name, syllable by syllable, but heard only the echo of her own voice in response. She became increasingly nervous and apprehensive, then wracked by real concern. Should she call Anne or Eric to tell them that their son had disappeared and that for once, she couldn't find him? No, she couldn't do that. If the police were to get involved, she would be questioned and they would discover that she didn't have a work permit.

Lolo went out into the garden. Perhaps Joseph was playing in the raspberry bushes, in spite of the rain. No luck. There was a yellow crane on the wet ground. Joseph must have left it there some time ago. She picked up the toy and felt like crying. "Where are you? Come back! You can't do this to me." She heard a noise. A truck was coming toward the house. It was Luis, the gardener. He pulled up to her and lowered the window. "What are you doing? Can't you see it's raining? You'll get sick if you're not careful!" Lolo explained that she was looking for Joseph and had already searched the house from top to bottom. She showed him the yellow toy.

"This is the only thing I could see. If you help me, maybe we can find him. I haven't told his parents. If I do, they'll call the police, and ..."

"I understand. Let's go back inside. He might have gone back in without your realizing."

Luis's voice was very reassuring. Lolo felt better.

They walked over to the house and took off their muddy shoes. Maybe the boy was just playing with one of his favorite robots in his bedroom. But nobody was there, and the toy had been tossed aside under a low chair. They searched every corner of the house, opening each door and calling the boy over and over. It was useless. "Let's ask our neighbors to help," Lolo said to Luis. "I'll take a photo of Joseph and show it to them. Perhaps they've seen him."

Suddenly, the telephone rang, and Lolo grabbed it. She couldn't place the voice immediately. Then she recognized it. "Hello, it's Carla Monte. I've got a little boy with me. He's soaked, but he doesn't seem to mind. It appears he was on an important mission: he came over to give me news from Madame Butterfly."

Relieved but also slightly bashful, Lolo replied, "I told him that he could make up the rest of the story."

"Well, that's exactly what he did. He thinks that Madame Butterfly left her family and went out walking in the rain. She carried on walking even though she didn't have an umbrella. Anyway, my visitor is waiting for you here. You can come and pick him up."

Luis took Lolo to the singers' house, a 1930s building barely visible through the trees. The gardener stayed in his truck while she ran over to the door. Carla was waiting for her, holding Joseph's hand. He ran toward Lolo, who kissed him and said a few words to him in Portuguese. She wanted to tell the boy and the singer how worried she had been, but she couldn't find the words, so she hurriedly thanked Carla and took Joseph over to the truck.

Luis put on his seat belt. Joseph fell fast asleep.

"So, all's well that ends well …"

"Not completely," Lolo said. "I still need you to help me."

"Sure, what do you need?"

"Can you take us to the airport?"

Luis was taken aback, but he asked no questions. He nodded and started down the road. The rain began again, drenching the buildings and slowing traffic. It ran down the window pane in rivulets, the windshield wipers ineffective. Lolo said nothing. Luis clutched the steering wheel with his callused hands.

"Are you OK? He's back now. Aren't you saying anything? You must have been really scared …"

Luis was right. Hunched over on the seat, her eyes lowered, the young woman was reliving the last few hours: the wet garden, the silence of the empty house, and the toys that Joseph had left behind. She couldn't stop thinking about what she would have said to his parents if she hadn't found the boy.

The throbbing noise of a low flying plane passed over the truck.

"So, what, you're going on a trip?" Luis asked.

"No, no, I just need a moment to dream before I go back to the house. Do you understand?"

"No, not really! But why not?" Luis asked, looking at the boy, who had just opened his eyes. "After all, kids love airplanes, right?"

At the drop-off area, the gardener helped Joseph out of the vehicle and gave him a wink.

"Make sure you hold on tight to Lolo's hand! Promise? I have to get going now. You're great company, but I've got work to do!"

Inside the building, Lolo showed the boy the board that listed the departures. Magical letters appeared. Rio de Janeiro. "See? Rio! That's where I come from." If she could, Lolo would take him up the hills around the city and show him the wide bay below. If they asked her any questions, she would tell people that Joseph was her son. The board made a series of clicking sounds, and other arrivals and departures appeared, with different times, different gates, and different names of cities, some unknown. In a low voice amidst the hubbub, a flight attendant asked all passengers flying to London to proceed immediately to Gate 19. Mr. Bertie

Salam, traveling to Mumbai, was informed that he had an urgent message.

Suddenly, Joseph forgot what he had been told, and let go of Lolo's hand. She started and tried to hold him back, but he was too quick for her, running straight ahead. In the crowd of passengers, he had recognized his grandparents walking slowly toward him, pushing a small suitcase on wheels. The child called them, and Aram saw him. "Joseph, *pasha*, what are you doing at the airport?" he asked. When he pronounced the Turkish word "*pasha*," his Armenian accent seemed to get stronger.

"We're looking for Madame Butterfly, *papig*," Joseph replied, earnestly. That was the term the young boy always called his grandfather.

"Wait, what happened to her?" Victoria asked, playing along. She understood Joseph's imagination. She would often join her grandson in his favorite game, following his orders and driving his yellow toy around, as he showed her how to dig a deep hole in the ground. Joseph would imitate the sound of the engine as Victoria operated the gears.

"Did Madame Butterfly leave the opera?" Aram asked in surprise.

Lolo smiled. She was happy to run into Aram and Victoria, who she didn't see that often. She knew how attached they were to the boy. For them, he represented the future of their exiled family. Sometimes, the grandparents would come for lunch on a Sunday. As she served the roast, Lolo would overhear snippets of conversation. Eric would always sit at the head of the table, polite but indifferent. He would open a bottle and pour a little wine into Aram's glass so that he could taste it and give his approval. Even though Anne rarely took Lolo into her confidence, one evening she had told her babysitter about Mehmet, as well as the scandal that had shaken the family when she announced her marriage and the subsequent relief that *hayrig* and *mayrig* felt when the Ottoman engagement was broken off. Lolo guessed that Mehmet's departure had inadvertently paved the way for Eric. Anne finished her story by saying, "From that moment on, my parents realized that I would be living my own life …" Lolo listened carefully to how Anoush had become Anne. She would have liked to meet Mehmet and hear his side of the story, to know if he had suffered, and to learn what had become of him. But Mehmet now lived in Istanbul, and Anne had apparently lost contact with him, although she failed to mention their recent meeting in the *café des Ormes*. All that remained, she said, were a few photos that she hadn't looked at for a long time. An awkward silence followed. Anne got up, went to the closet, and took out a small box made of cherry wood. She opened it. Underneath some folded papers there was a photo of a slim young man with dark hair, smiling shyly. Anne examined the photo as if she had never seen it before, then put it back. Lolo had a lot of questions, but she understood that this was not the right time to ask.

As they walked through the concourse, Joseph pulled on his grandfather's sleeve.

"*Papig*, can you help me to find Madame Butterfly?"

"Of course, *pasha*, but she may have gone through customs," Aram said, pointing towards passport control.

"She must already be on the plane," said Lolo, going one step further. She looked at the clock on the information board. "We should be getting back now. We need to get home before your parents, or they'll be worried."

The boy leapt into his grandfather's arms. He was strong and protective. "Carry me! I'm tired." Aram asked Lolo if they could share a taxi home.

Back home and safely tucked up in bed, Joseph asked Lolo, "Do you really think that Madame Butterfly took a plane?"

"Yes, but don't worry. She'll definitely be back."

The boy fell into a deep sleep. His parents had still not come home.

A few years later, just before his twelfth birthday, Joseph was alone in the house on the edge of the lake when the phone rang. It took him a minute to recognize Lolo's voice, which he hadn't heard for a long time. The young woman on the other end of the line spoke hesitantly, and when she couldn't find the right word, switched to Portuguese. She asked Joseph if he still understood her, and he reassured her. Listening to her sing-song way of speaking, he was overcome by emotion. He had become very close to Lolo, but had then been abruptly separated from her years ago. A memory, fixed firmly in his mind, took him back to that moment when he got up to find his mother alone in the kitchen. She gave him a cup of chocolate and said, "There's no rice pudding today. Lolo isn't here anymore, and I'm not sure she is coming back. We'll spend the day together today, OK? I'm not going to work. Tomorrow, your father and I will find someone else." There was no explanation, nothing to rationalize the feeling of abandonment that came over him. How could his parents even conceive of a replacement for Lolo, who sang Brazilian lullabies to him when she put him to bed? Lolo, who would call out for him when he hid behind the shrubs in the garden? Adults didn't understand a thing.

An English woman with an oval-shaped head and a twisted chignon eventually took over "instead of Lolo," as Eric told his son offhandedly. On her first day, the new woman asked Joseph to call her "Miss Dorothy." He complied, but tried to say her name as little as possible. Food was a serious problem. Joseph was horrified by the vegetable mush that Miss Dorothy served him up day after day. He could not understand why she always chose the hardest, most tasteless carrots she could find. She had been warned that the child liked to hide in certain corners of the house or behind the shrubs, and so she followed Joseph's parents' instructions and would look for him half-heartedly, but give up quickly, going to the laundry to iron Anne's multicolored collection of silk blouses instead. Luis couldn't get used to Miss Dorothy either. Like Joseph, he missed Lolo, with her dark skin and nice figure. When he got to the house, he would jump out of his truck, tools in hand, and call out, "Hey, Ireland!" when he spotted Miss Dorothy. She would remind him that she was English. "Whatever, it's still an island!" he would reply mischievously. Her face pink and expressionless, Miss Dorothy turned away, indifferent. She was unflappable, and her calm demeanor allowed her to deal both with Joseph's polite hostility and Anne and Eric's tumultuous arguments.

"And your parents?" Lolo asked. "How are they?"

"Well, they fight a lot," Joseph quickly replied. "In the evening, they shout at one another in the living room, and I can hear them from my room." He changed the subject. "Where are you now?"

"I came back home, to Rio."

"I didn't understand why you left. You didn't tell me you were going."

"No, my dearest," Lolo said, addressing him just like she used to. "I had no time to warn you."

"You could have at least told me you were leaving …"

"I would have loved to, but the police didn't give me any time."

The young woman was hesitant to go into too much detail because she didn't want to alarm the boy. But she also knew that Joseph deserved the truth, so she started telling him the circumstances of her departure. One morning at dawn, no doubt alerted by a nosy neighbor, the police knocked on the door of the small apartment Lolo shared with a friend. Alone at the time and half asleep, Lolo saw the men in uniform and immediately understood that she was trapped. Unable to produce a visa, she had to admit to having overstayed her legal presence in the country. After they had demanded her cell phone, the police bombarded Lolo with questions, but she refused to say where she worked. If she had let on, Anne and Eric Landolt would have been issued with a huge fine. Cool but courteous, the police ordered Lolo to gather her personal effects and follow them. Sirens blaring, they took her to the airport where she liked to go with Joseph. They locked her up in a building that was called the "Welcome Center," a euphemism that was not lost on her. Two days later, she was involuntarily put on a plane back to Brazil. Lolo took a final glance at Lake Geneva, which looked like a blue cloth. She felt profoundly unwelcome. "There is no place for me," she thought.

"You know, I would have loved to stay with you, but I wasn't given any choice. I was thrown out," Lolo said, finishing her story.

"And what are you doing now?" Joseph asked. His voice was breaking, and it went up and down.

"I take care of a German boy called Wolf. His parents have been in Brazil for three years. They work in an international company. I go to their house every day, cook for them and wash their clothes."

"How old is this Wolf?"

"The same age as you. Twelve."

"I hate him," Joseph said. He had found a rival on the other side of the world.

"Ah, don't be jealous … it's pointless."

"Why is it pointless?"

"You're my only Joseph. There will never be another."

"Well, that's lucky, because I have a plan to get you

back. Want to hear it?"

"Tell me …"

"In a few years, we'll get married, so prepare to dump Wolf."

Lolo burst out laughing.

"OK, excellent idea! And for our wedding, we'll ask a singer to sing the tune from Madame Butterfly. Do you remember?"

"Wait, I forgot. What was that again?"

"Madame Butterfly disappeared, and you went off to look for her."

"Oh yes, now I remember. You couldn't find me, and you were really worried, right?"

"Yes, I was. I didn't know what to tell your family. Do you still like music?"

"I've been playing cello for three years. It's my favorite instrument. It's like my friend. When you come back to Geneva, I'll play it for you. Just for you."

Lolo acquiesced. "He's grown up, but he's still the same," she thought. "I recognize him, even though his voice is changing."

"And your grandparents? You haven't spoken of them …"

"They're getting older, but they're well. My *papig* had a weird idea. He wants me to learn Armenian."

"Why not? When will you begin?"

Joseph explained to Lolo that he didn't want to learn the language of his distant ancestors. He had been surprised by Aram's suggestion, because Aram had never wanted his own children to speak or write in Armenian. And now he seemed to think that this legacy, since it was in danger of disappearing, could simply skip a generation and be handed over to his one grandson.

"Did you tell him what you thought?" Lolo asked.

"Not really. I don't want to hurt him, so I make up

excuses. Like … I'll say that I've got too much school work, or that I want to learn Russian. Oh, and I've also got my cello, which takes up a lot of time. I find whatever excuse I can!"

They spoke for a long time, like two accomplices that had reunited. They said goodbye several times, but neither managed to hang up. When the conversation started to fade, it would suddenly come alive again. The memories resurfaced and brought the past back to life.

VIII

The Life of a Writer

Anne and Eric's relationship continued to deteriorate as time went by despite the fondness that they still had for one another. Small details got to them, no matter how meaningless they were. For example, after flooding the bathroom when taking a shower, Eric would act as if nothing had happened. Anne, extremely finicky about her nails, would apply polish stroke after stroke, her head held rigidly as she leant back with a dissatisfied look. They did not understand the exact reasons for the gradual distancing that was developing between them by the day, but sadly, there was a kind of remoteness that they could not ignore. The one who paid the price was Joseph, now an adolescent.

They took advantage of a short vacation to get away from their house on Lake Geneva. Some friends had loaned them a cabin in the Alps, with a brief invitation that papered over the implicit message: "Go on, it'll do you good." It was an area of impressive scenery, far from the prettied-up villages frequented by the rich and famous, and it offered a 360° view of the mountain range, which stretched away in the distance as far as the eye could see. The peaks sparkled in the late autumn light, each one distinct. The dark wood cabin, built into the slope, was surrounded by the last of the larches that could grow at that high altitude, and the trees seemed to cast a protective golden shadow over the house. The calm and beauty of the place lifted their spirits at first, but tension soon grew between them. The simplest pretext would give rise to an argument (like an interminable debate about whether or not to buy a new car). It would be intense and pointless, come to a head, stop, start again, and seemingly never finish. Round and round they went, with the same quarrels, the same reproaches. During the brief intervals when his parents eased up, Joseph, hiding behind a comic, hoped that the silence would transport him elsewhere. Yet each time, he was disappointed. He took refuge in his reading, using it as his defense. But one evening, when he could no longer deal with his parents' aggressive behavior, he slammed his book shut and threw it on the floor so violently that it flew across the room. Then he got up and knocked over a chair, shouting, "You make me sick, the pair of you! You're like two children insulting one another! Shut up! I'm going to practice the cello."

Anne and Eric were stunned by this unusual outburst. Caught unawares, they realized that their son had grown up in front of their very eyes. Without forewarning, Joseph was no longer a child, and from now on, even though they did not realize it, they would need to take his opinions and judgment into account. When he talked to his parents, he made juddering, awkward movements, pulling down on his shirt sleeves, which had grown too short. He ran his fingers through his tousled hair as if he were trying to reassure himself. Eric was red in the face.

"Is that how you talk to us? Who do you think you are? You think you're going to teach us a lesson, or what?" he asked. He felt as though his authority were being questioned. "Your mother and I are having an argument, that's it. If you're not happy, you can go out for a walk. Understand?"

"Listen, papa, you're not having an argument. You've been fighting for an hour," Joseph replied. "I'm sick of it. That's all."

"That's no reason for you to kick over a chair. Put it back, right now."

"Pick it up yourself if you feel like it."

"If I feel like it? What? Talk to me properly. I'm your

father, not one of your classmates."

"Don't worry, there's no way I'll get that mixed up."

"Joseph, stop talking back. You've gone way over the line. I'll throw you out if you carry on!"

Father and son, now the same height, looked at each other defiantly. "That boy will be bigger than Eric soon," Anne thought. She intervened.

"That's enough. It's all over now, so let's calm down. Look, why don't you make up? I'll pick up the chair. There are no winners or losers here."

"Leave that chair alone," Eric barked, furiously. "If not, our young friend will tip over the table tomorrow. You obviously don't understand a thing …"

The tone with which his father said "our young friend" hurt Joseph all the more, because he couldn't think of anything to reply. Once again, he was relegated to his role as a little boy being taught a lesson. Tears welled up in his eyes. He wanted to hide his fear at all costs, in case it was seen as a weakness. So, he grabbed his jacket and went out, the upturned chair still lying on the floor.

In huge strides, Joseph took a path along a stream. It was cool by the running water. Little by little, he calmed down, even though he kept going over the scene in his head. Other thoughts crept into his mind, and he could not help but reach an inevitable conclusion. "They're going to break up, I'm sure. I need to be careful not to get caught up in their mess. I wonder what they'll do with the house. I don't want to move. I've always lived there, and it's my house too! I can see it now. They'll each go their own way and play at being those modern parents who ask their child which parent he wants to live with."

Night fell. He was tempted to stay outdoors, just to make Anne and Eric fret about him. He wanted to use his absence to show his parents how tormented he was by the feelings of rage and disappointment they had caused him to have. He wondered if they would try to find him when he didn't come home, or if they would call the police. He couldn't stop thinking about how immature they were, but he eventually pushed those thoughts aside and turned to go home. Why should he sleep outside anyway, under the trees or behind the woodshed? Definitely not because of grownups and their conflicts…"It's their problem. Not mine," he decided. When he opened the door to the cabin, he was relieved to see that everything had calmed down. Eric was preparing dinner. He had put the meat in the oven and was cutting the vegetables into small pieces, while Anne, tucked up on the sofa, was reading a detective novel. Joseph got the cello out of its case and started playing. He leaned his instrument toward him, and they formed a duo, almost as close as two lovers. The notes spread deep and wide across the room. They rose to the beams, and bounced back. Dancing through the open window, they left the cabin to join the mountains.

Two weeks later, Joseph was absorbed in a homework assignment, even though it was already midnight. He looked disheveled. "I'll never finish this," he thought, "and tomorrow morning that brute Morel is going to tear me apart in front of the whole class." It wasn't that Louis-Auguste Morel, his renowned French teacher, used corporal punishment, but his sarcastic teaching style could hit just like body blows. His students feared him, but they hid their apprehension carefully behind an adolescent façade of noisy laughter and sarcastic gestures, and that was how they defended themselves against this unpredictable teacher. Louis-Auguste Morel was a distant relative of a portrait artist who had painted the children of the tsar, a fact of which he reminded his students more often than necessary. Depending on the day, he could be chatty and lighthearted, but other times he would coil up behind his desk, eyes half closed, ready to shoot an arrow at whatever victim took his fancy. He made certain of his authority in class by dint of his capricious moods. Any would-be disagreement or even worse, challenge, was immediately nipped in the bud. Even the parents, so swift to defend their offspring, were silent in the face of this man that they considered, wrongly of course, to be a paragon of pedagogy.

The homework Louis-Auguste Morel had assigned was the terse essay assignment "The Life of a Writer." It caused great perplexity among the students. Were they supposed to summarize the life of a famous person? To obediently complete the notes that they'd taken during the previous class? Or could they, as Joseph wanted to do, simply let their imaginations run wild with fictitious characters? When asked the question, LAM (named thus by previous generations of students) had replied, "Ladies and Gentlemen, if I understand it correctly, you are now seniors in high school. Therefore, you are no longer in kindergarten. I'll let you make your own minds up." He snapped his satchel shut and left the room, no doubt determined to continue his fight against the "childish direction of secondary education," whose destructive effects he hated with a passion. The principal, unfortunately, paid no attention to his dire warnings.

Clémence Dumas was a short, dark-haired girl with a lively temperament. She leant over toward Joseph and muttered, "Sadistic old man! He's worse than a bulldog! I'll let you make your own minds up," she added, imitating the teacher. Joseph smiled. Clémence was pretty, and the two of them would often go to a bakery in the old town after class and get themselves a hot chocolate. To hide his shyness, the boy would state confidently, "I'll leave my bike here and go with you," hoping that he would be able to muster the courage to take her hand and pull her toward him.

The teacher was intrigued by the surname Dumas, and tried to find out if she was the descendant of a genius. The poor student shook her head in barely concealed exasperation. "What a pity!" Louis-Auguste Morel reacted, as if overwhelmed by disappointment. "You could have shown us your documents or told us some stories." Joseph could understand how annoying it was to have everyone ask you the same question over and over ("Dumas, like Alexander?") He scrawled a note on a piece of paper and gave it to her. "Tell him that you have the manuscript of *The Three Musketeers* on a bookcase in your living room!"

He set himself to addressing this open-ended assignment from Mr. Morel and decided to make up a story about a young woman who bore a surprising resemblance to Clémence. His character had written a scandalous novel when she was young, a mixture of prose and comic strip, and an editor fell in love with it (or maybe he had fallen in love with her). An aggressive publicity campaign had thrust the novel into the limelight. A 21st century "Sagan" had been born, and within a few weeks, a portrait of the young prodigy appeared on the side of buses and in bookstore windows. Then there was a year of TV programs, book signings in far-flung places, and translation rights from one end of Europe to the other. But the waters of fame began to recede as more and more questions arose. Was there going to be a second book? What was it to be about? When would it be published? Or was the first book just a flash in the pan? etc. Put in the hot seat like this, the young woman found a shoulder to lean on (a love interest, more than a friend), in a guy that she'd known for a few years. He assured her of his support, and even gave her some sound advice. Thanks to him, she was able to write a new novel, so despite the dire predictions, her second book was likewise a great success.

It was very late by the time Joseph had finished his homework, correcting all the typos, punctuation and spelling mistakes. He read the text again, this time out loud, something he would have to do when called on in class. He was still not satisfied, so he tried to change the order of the paragraphs, take out certain phrases and rework the conclusion. He began to sweat. He couldn't completely redo a story that he had worked so hard on, particularly not at the eleventh hour, so he decided to stop there. "'The Life of a Writer': what a stupid prompt!" he muttered, before dozing off.

The next morning, Joseph put on a clean shirt (Louis-Auguste Morel would no doubt notice this detail and would give him extra points for it) and waited to be called on. When he was summoned ("Your turn, Joseph Landolt"), he went up to the blackboard and read his fictitious biography in a voice that sounded less self-assured than he would have liked. From time to time, he looked up at Clémence Dumas. She was listening. At the end of the story, she began to smile and made a slight gesture with her hand. She had recognized herself.

Joseph finished, but the students didn't say a word. Louis-Auguste Morel, wearing a black jacket a little too small for his portly figure, turned toward Clémence.

"Miss Dumas, I think you liked Joseph's story, right? If I'm not mistaken, you've even been trying to attract his attention… So, go on, give us your opinion."

"He did really well," Clémence said seriously.

"Explain further. Tell us what you think, please."

"It's a lively and well-written description. You can imagine what that young girl was going through when her novel was so successful."

"Do you think the story is really plausible? Could the reader believe it, even for an instant?"

"Yes, of course, these things do happen. For example…"

Clémence made the mistake of talking about an adolescent singer who had become famous overnight after she posted a short clip of her work online. Louis-Auguste Morel pounced.

"Thank you, Miss Dumas. That is exactly what I wanted to hear. We were served up with a banal story to which we could all easily relate because of its trendy style. Yet it had no depth or permanence. No reader is going to swallow this concoction. It lacks taste and character."

"You asked me for my opinion," Clémence replied, disguising her anger. "I liked the story! I would even like to hear it over again." Trying to get the rest of the class to back her up, she added, "And I'm not the only one…"

"You have all the rights in the world to give us your appraisal," the teacher replied dryly. "However, I don't wish to hear you speaking for everyone else."

Joseph was still standing in front of the class, a silent witness to this conversation. He was bombarded by two distinct feelings: disappointment, at hearing Louis-Auguste Morel tearing his work apart, and a delicious pleasure at hearing Clémence back him so vigorously. The teacher's voice cut through, as if out of a mist.

"I'm sorry to tell you, Mr. Landolt, that your story is unsatisfactory. You usually write well, and I commend you for that. But this time, you have failed miserably, regardless of what Clémence thinks. Her arguments in your favor don't seem very pertinent, even though I must admit she appeared to speak with conviction."

Louis-Auguste Morel paused and cast a glance at the two adolescents. Then he continued:

"Joseph, I'll let you do your homework over. You can give me your new assignment next week. Don't write fiction, or you'll retreat into a web of clichés again. Just write the biography of a writer who actually exists. I'm sure your work will be better. OK, that's all for today. You can go. See you next Monday."

The students filed out. Joseph wanted to get out of there, so he was one of the first to leave. He was furious at being forced to start from scratch. He was just about to get on his bike when he heard Clémence's voice.

"Hey, don't run off so quickly. Wait for me! I can't keep up."

He turned around and smiled.

"Thank you for your help. I really appreciate it…"

"I wasn't too helpful actually. I thought of other things to say, but it was too late. Morel wasn't going to let me talk any more. I should have tried harder."

"Well, maybe he was right. Nobody's going to believe my story."

"What? Are you joking? Don't tell me you agree with that idiot!"

"I took too long to get started. At midnight, I was still writing, but I couldn't concentrate. I should have…"

"Don't be silly," Clémence interrupted. "Anyway, that young woman you were describing, I think she sounds great!"

"Really? Me too," Joseph said, pushing his bicycle with his right hand.

He slowed down and moved over toward Clémence, brushing her shoulder. He leaned toward her, and without thinking, in the most natural way possible, searched for her lips. He had time to think, "She looks like a strawberry! I really like her…" They both closed their eyes, their hearts beating.

Aram was lonely. The year before, he had lost his wife to a heart attack. So, when he learned about the problems in

Joseph's family, he suggested that the boy go and live with him for a while. "*Pasha*, a change of scenery will do you good. You can keep me company, and make me coffee in the morning." The boy's parents were reluctant at first, but eventually they agreed. Actually, they were relieved. Joseph got some clothes together, stuffed his books into a backpack and went to live with his grandfather, who had just moved to the country. Aram had invested in a quirky old house, which backed onto a turret. He was happy to have his only grandchild come and live with him. There was a strong bond between Aram and Joseph, and they had gotten through a lot of the family conflicts together. Aram was very fond of the boy. Their relationship was different from the one he had with his children, Anne and Arthur.

Joseph carried the weight of all Aram's expectations for the future, and as he got older, he became the custodian of his hopes. His grandfather's face was engraved with the temperament of a survivor. He had fled from danger, destruction and massacre, and he would forever carry the memory of those atrocities with him. His past was chiseled into his consciousness, although he rarely spoke of it, as if he feared that by articulating the words, he would bring back past sufferings. He had lost the innocence of youth forever. The terror he felt when his parents were assassinated had morphed into a feeling of invincibility. He had built a rampart to protect himself so that from now on, nothing could destroy him because he was beyond the reach of danger. He wanted to turn this power over to Joseph, this grandson who as a child was constantly hiding behind the living room curtains. But Joseph had now grown up. When he reached for the bow of his cello, he grasped it firmly.

When Joseph returned from school, Aram immediately noticed he looked different.

"What's wrong? You look agitated. Your hair looks like a battlefield!"

"Oh yes?" Joseph replied. "No, it's nothing, I promise."
"*Pasha*, I don't believe you. Something's happened."
Joseph smiled, but said nothing.
"Let me guess," Aram continued. "Wait…"
"*Papig*, leave me alone."
"I think I can guess! You want to know what I think?"
"Not really. Well, maybe. Try me."
"You, my boy, are in love."
"Hey! How do you know?"
"You don't need glasses to see that! What's her name? Well, you don't have to tell me if you don't want to…"

"Clémence. She's in my class. We sit next to each other."
"I'm sure she's pretty."
"Yes, she is," Joseph said, blushing. "This morning, she stuck up for me in French class."
"Did you need to be defended?"

Joseph told Aram about his essay and how his teacher hadn't liked it. He described how Clémence had taken his side.

"She stood up to Morel's criticism, but it wasn't enough. I have to do the homework over and give it in next week."
"Are you going to make up a new story?"
"No, this time, I have to base my story on the life of a writer who actually existed, and I really don't want to."
"Do you have any ideas yet?"
"Perhaps Vladimir N."
"Vladimir N? Who are you talking about?"
"Nabokov. He used to live near here, in a hotel on Lake Geneva."
"Oh, of course, he's an important figure. But I've got another idea. What about an Armenian writer?"
"Impossible," Joseph replied. "I have no idea about them, and I wouldn't know who to pick."
"Well, it's time you learned. I can help you if you want."

"Can you think of anyone?"

"You might look at Zabel Essayan. She was an incredible woman who was born near Constantinople."

"Constantinople?"

"Byzantium, if you prefer. Today, it's called Istanbul."

"Did she stay in the city?"

"No, first she went to France, and then she went back to the Ottoman Empire."

"…to become a novelist?"

Aram talked about the works that Zabel Essayan had put together in a book titled *In the Ruins*. She wrote about her trips throughout the Ottoman Empire and described what she had seen in 1909 in Adana, when thousands of Armenians were killed.

"Was the book ever translated?" Joseph asked. He wasn't particularly interested in the topic, and hoped his grandfather would say no.

"Yes, it's easy to find. I can buy it for you if you like."

"I don't know, *papig*. It sounds a little heavy, don't you think?"

"Well, yes, that's true. Even more so because Zabel disappeared during Stalin's Great Purge."

"Wow, that's really dark: death, ruin, disappearance. What's left? To be honest, I'm not sure that…"

"I understand, but it's our history, even if you don't want to hear it."

"That's it," Joseph said, more harshly than he meant. "So what, now tell me. I'm afraid."

"And what if you are?" Aram asked.

Joseph did not reply. He looked at his grandfather's furrowed face. He did not want to disappoint him, but at the same time, the tragic events described by Zabel Essayan seemed so remote that he actually found them immaterial. Of course he knew that he was a distant heir to that story, but at this point, the line of descent had been broken and lost.

How could he explain that to Aram without hurting him? How could he tell him that the ruins of Zabel Essayan had disappeared? That they had been swallowed by time, and covered with forgetful and ungrateful silence? Perhaps survivors found it necessary to forget. "He's right," Joseph thought. "It's true - I am afraid, and I can't admit it." He had chosen to make up a biography for his assignment, comfortably distant from reality and the nightmares of the past. Inspired by Clémence, he had blissfully built a castle in the sky, painting a picture of a fictional character who found success without having sought it out. Now, however, his teacher's sharp criticism had unexpectedly placed a courageous Armenian writer in Joseph's path. A vision of Clémence came into his mind. "I'll see her again tomorrow…" The emotion, and desire too, sent shivers down his spine.

"What are you thinking about?" Aram asked.

"Oh, nothing," Joseph replied, evasively.

"You can choose whatever topic you like. Take Vladimir N. if you prefer. Besides, he was also an exile… I think I have *Lolita* in my library."

Aram said nothing more. He settled comfortably into his armchair, put on the light, and opened up his paper.

The horses whinnied, rearing up in a cloud of dust. The young woman in the saddle looked up. The city on the horizon was on fire. Two dark clouds of smoke rose out of the flames. It was midday, but the sky was growing darker and darker, as if a giant eclipse had chased the day away. The boy who accompanied the visitor blinked and looked scared. He suggested that they go back. "We can't keep going in this direction. It's too dangerous," he said, speaking in Turkish. Zabel Essayan was emotionless. She refused to yield. She was going to Adana to take care of the wounded and maybe save them. She wanted to see for herself what was happening and let the whole world know. Now that she was so close, it was out of the question for her to give up. "You go if you want. I'll continue without you." The boy looked at her, at a loss for words. He understood that it was impossible to sway her from her goal, but despite his promise to carry on, fear won out. He opened the grey canvas bag slung over his shoulder and gave Zabel the few remaining provisions it contained: a flask of lukewarm water, some figs, and a slice of unleavened bread. Tugging on the reins, he held back the bony mare. He spat on the ground and then retraced his steps. It was as if he was disgusted with himself.

Zabel Essayan drew close to the inferno and arrived in front of a half-demolished building. The wall above the entrance was partly cracked, which had left a gaping hole. It was in danger of collapse. Sections of the roof had been torn away and were strewn across the floor, and kitchen utensils and wooden toys were scattered indiscriminately. Zabel was slender yet elegant, despite the dust covering her clothes. She got off the horse and secured it to a tree. Then she went into the ruins, where the silence was complete. She took out a notebook from her pocket to jot down some ideas for a newspaper article back in Constantinople. Then, suddenly, she heard a noise, and a child emerged from the darkness. He was about five years old, and filthy. Tattered rags covered his body, and he looked at her as if she were a ghost. She decided not to go forward so as not to frighten him, but instead reached out her arms and smiled. At first, he didn't move either, but then he walked toward her. She saw that he had a cut on his face, so she took out a linen handkerchief and tried to clean him up. Gently, she asked him in Armenian if he was alone. He sniffed, and replied, "Yes, they've all gone. They got taken away." Zabel understood that something terrible had happened, so she didn't question him further. She tried to push away the feelings of sadness and powerlessness that invaded her thoughts. She took the child by the hand, leading him to a well that she had seen when she arrived. She sat on the edge and lowered the bucket, filling it with cool water. Then she took a section of her dress, wet it, and washed the child's swollen face. She found a fig in her knapsack and peeled it. The boy grabbed it eagerly, putting the whole thing into his mouth. Behind him, in the distance, the city was still burning.

It was dawn. Joseph woke up. "Up you get," he said to himself. "*Papig* needs his coffee."

Joseph opened his blue notebook.

Zabel, I did not want to meet you, but you came out of the darkness toward me, so powerful and so convincing. Your shadow appeared on the wall of my bedroom. I would have liked to tame my fear, talk to you, listen to you, but I didn't dare. What happened to the boy you found in the ruins of his house? Did you save him? Did he run away, like a fugitive among the dead?

Zabel, when I turned on the lamp, you had disappeared. The boy, too. It was just me, alone in the bedroom.

Harry Koumrouyan

IX

The Fruit Basket

Would Anne and Eric Landolt separate "by mutual agreement" (a euphemism that concealed their bitter resentment)? Would they believe they were trapped, stuck in a rut, with the happy moments fewer and farther in between? Or would they be able to sort out some kind of working relationship? The future seemed blurry. They couldn't envisage what was to come. When they were together, they tore each other apart, yet alone they sought each other out. Nothing seemed possible, neither the status quo nor a change.

One evening, when they believed they were alone in the house, Eric took out a bottle of whiskey and offered Anne a drink. She accepted.

"Are we celebrating our divorce?" she asked, seemingly casual. "In some cultures, they celebrate all the rites of passage, even the sad ones."

"Oh yes?" asked Eric, as if the comment hadn't gotten to him. "I never heard of that custom. In that case, let's take out the best bottle. Do you want ice?"

"No, thanks. I prefer it straight up."

Eric took out some long glasses. As he poured the drinks, he looked at Anne, who had lit a cigarette. Watching her exhale, he was seized by a breath of desire, which bothered him. "She's still very pretty," he thought. Brushing her hand, he held out the glass, and made a move to sit next to her.

"Can I?"

He pointed to the sofa.

"Eric, let's sit facing one another. That would make it easier to talk."

151

"Too late," he announced, plopping down beside her.

"He's incorrigible," she thought. He smiled. The dimples in his cheeks made him look younger, and Anne thought back to their first meeting. He had been run over by a reckless driver at a congested intersection, and they had carried him on a stretcher to the clinic where she was on duty. He had hurt his shoulder, but he quickly snapped out of it and made light of the injury. She understood at that time that he didn't want to appear vulnerable. Of course, the accident had made him weak, but he tried to hide it, and recovered quickly. She remembered that moment in precise detail: the blue shirt he was wearing (a particular label with a logo on the pocket, which had been torn when he was thrown off the bike); the stubby fingers of the police officer writing up the report; the bicycle with the buckled wheel that had been wrenched off the axle. "To think that it took a traffic accident for us to meet!"

And then there was silence.

"Shall we toast? To us and our futures."

Trying his best to act cheerful, he replied,

"OK, cheers!"

That evening (the evening of "great explanations," as Eric baptized it, half seriously), they went into the living room, where they would often sit after dinner, drinking black coffee together in silence. Over the years, they had furnished the room with keepsakes that complemented each other even though at first glance they appeared rather disparate. Every purchase brought back a memory, a moment they had spent together, trinkets acquired during their trips and carefully transported back home. In Berlin, they'd bought a lamp whose polished glass and steel base cast a pleasant glow on the low table next to the sofa. An Oriental rug covered the entire length of the parquet floor. It had intertwined motifs and had been given to them by Anne's parents a few Christmases ago. Aram always knew how to put his own spin on things, and said, "I don't know where this rug comes from, but if you agree, we can decide that it was woven in Armenia. I can assure you, that's plausible. Just look at the designs and the colors."

Eric pointed at the furniture and the paintings around him, singling out one particular lithography he liked very much.

"It's crazy that we're leaving this beautiful place and selling the house. Luckily, we'll always have photos. We can make an album. That should bring back some nice memories."

"Now you're getting sentimental. You've reached the stage of regret?"

"Well, why not? I'm not a robot. You're telling me it makes no difference to you whether you leave or not?"

"Of course not. Still, I think it's for the best. And plus…"

"We can change our minds at any time," Eric interrupted. "There's no obligation to leave. It's not too late."

"What are you playing at? Yesterday, you agreed we should separate. You even thought it was a good idea, and you said you were going to consult a lawyer."

"So what? I can change my mind, can't I? Only fools don't change their minds… You know the saying!"

"Yes, I know how it goes. But there's one other thing. You're not the only one that makes decisions. You forget that there are two of us."

Eric adopted a conciliatory tone.

"I know, I know. But tell me, do you really want me to disappear from your life like that, boom, finished, adiós?"

"You're not going to vanish into thin air, you know that."

"Oh yes, and why not?"

"Joseph. Don't you remember that we have a son together?"

"So? Just like in the movies, the young lad and mommy go off together, arm in arm, and the father disappears.

Everybody knows the storyline. I'll never see you again."

"Joseph is fifteen. He's old enough to have his own opinions, and I'm telling you that nobody will ever ask him to choose between us. Never, you understand?"

Eric gave Anne a doubtful glance, then got up and opened the window. A gentle breeze came into the room, lifting the curtains. You could see the calm waters of Lake Geneva in the distance. The sparkling lights of the buildings opposite shimmered on its surface.

Eric came back over to the sofa and stood behind the backrest. He stroked the velvet covering, and then, slowly, began to caress Anne's shoulders. Neither of them moved. For a moment, there was complete silence. Then, he bent over, putting his lips on her neck and smelling her skin. She did not move, and they hugged.

At that very moment, Joseph came out of his room. He had come home earlier than expected. He heard the conversation through the open door, and approached the living room. He leaned against the wall in the hallway, unseen, afraid of disturbing this rare moment of intimacy. He was shocked, then hesitant, then hopeful. "I wonder what's going on," he thought. "They fight, they make up, they fight again. They never stop."

Joseph followed the movements of his father attentively. He was now sitting back on the sofa, to Anne's left.

"I have one question," Eric said.

"You still have questions? I thought you'd already asked me everything."

"Your Ottoman fiancé, I forget his name… what happened to him?"

Anne sat up.

"Don't tell me that you're going to talk about Mehmet this evening. It's not the time or the place."

"Why not?"

"Mehmet has nothing to do with you and me. Absolutely nothing."

"I'm not so sure about that."

"What on earth are you talking about? Are you out of your mind? Mehmet wasn't even in my life any more when I met you. You know that!"

"Yes, but he was still there. Just admit it. You've never forgotten him."

"My goodness, you're so jealous," Anne said, trying to hide her contentment. "So what?"

"He was the one you wanted to marry, but admit it, you gave in to your parents. They just couldn't imagine their dear, perfect daughter, etc., etc., marrying an Ottoman. To them, it was simply impossible. You knew it, so you left him and you've always regretted it. Then I showed up, but I had no chance. I could never replace him because he was always *there*."

Eric pointed at Anne's heart as he said the word 'there.' She took a step back.

"You're oversimplifying things. My parents did meddle where they weren't wanted, that's true, but I was the one who decided to break up with Mehmet. It wasn't them. Armenian women are free to do their own thing too, you know." (Eric shrugged, as if he'd heard it all before.) "Why would you think otherwise? Right after we broke up, Mehmet went back home. We moved on."

Anne repeated, more loudly, "We moved on." But Eric kept pushing the point.

"Really? Are you sure? Because I always get the impression that he's still prowling around between us."

"You're inventing a rivalry that doesn't exist. Why do you keep going back to the past? I didn't even know you then. Please Eric, I don't feel like dragging up old memories tonight."

"Old memories," Eric continued, looking straight at Anne. "So… you haven't seen him again, your Ottoman?"

The question took Anne by surprise, and she wanted to put an end to the conversation. She propped herself up on the cushions, trying to look as determined as she could.

"Leave Mehmet alone. Let's talk about something else…"

"First, answer my question."

"I don't understand what you're playing at."

"I'm not playing. It's serious. You're not going to tell me?"

Anne looked at Eric. He had lost his domineering attitude. His eyes were misty. She knew this air of fragility, and was touched. She gave in.

"Yes, I did see him. But only once. He was passing through Geneva, and we met up in the *café des Ormes*, a bistro where we used to get together."

"And?"

"Then he totally surprised me…"

Anne started to tell Eric how her Ottoman fiancé had discovered his grandmother's real identity.

"You can imagine how shocked I was. You get brought up with the image of the enemy, and you're convinced that the world is divided between the virtuous and the wicked. You've made a clean break with your country. The history books deceive you, and so do the official statements. And then one day, the truth catches up with you in your own family. It's as if an inferno had burned all the way up to your own house. And as for Mehmet, well, when he heard his grandmother's story, all the pretenses disappeared. In a few hours, she broke the silence of a lifetime. Her story sent him into a tailspin."

"Wait, but I'm missing something. That same grandson was ready to marry a girl from the opposite camp. Where's the logic in that?"

"I imagine that Mehmet felt free in Geneva. It's neutral terrain, far from the battlegrounds. The distance no doubt helped him to break free from the past. Things suddenly seemed so simple."

"You spoke about it, though?"

"Not too much, in the end. We were in our own bubble…"

"… until your parents burst the bubble. And what about Mehmet's parents? What did they make of it all?"

"He did send photos to Istanbul, but he never actually told his family about me. He said we were both students, but hid the rest."

"So he was lying by omission."

"Exactly. That was the easiest thing to do."

After she said this, Anne got up and went over to the open window. She leaned out, breathing in the smell of the flowers and the grass. Her back turned, she hoped that the questions would stop coming.

"Wait," Eric said, "I'd like to know the whole story."

"That's enough. We're closing the book on Mehmet. Why are you so curious all of a sudden? It's a bit strange, you know."

"Not at all. It's about time I understood the conflict between your two peoples."

"Stop interrogating me. Read a history book. You don't require my explanation, and plus, my business with Mehmet isn't going to give you any clues. It's just my life…"

"You're wrong. I know how the Ottoman Empire shred everything to pieces, how it tried to wipe out different populations… I know all that. It's the big Story with a capital S. But today, what's left? And what are the consequences for its descendants? You got stuck in the upheaval with your fiancé from Istanbul, and no matter what you say, you dragged me in your wake. Don't you understand?"

Anne sat down again. She shook her dark hair.

"I'm tired," she said. "Let's talk about this some other time."

"You need a top-up," Eric said, pouring his wife another glass of whisky.

"Listen," Anne said, "you're mixing everything up, but if you insist, I'll tell you what happened. After that, you're going to have to drop it. You'll understand why."

This declaration took Eric aback. What was he about to discover? "You live with someone for years," he thought, "you love this person, she takes you into her confidence, she reveals herself to you, but she still keeps things from you, things that she doesn't say. You can never know the whole story."

Joseph stood motionless in the dark corridor, his hands in the pockets of his patched-up jeans. He listened to his parents with a growing sense of curiosity and bewilderment. He wondered where this figure of Mehmet and his grandmother had come from. On the eve of their separation (if he was to believe the announcement that they had made to him), there was definitely some tension between Anne and Eric, yet they had never seemed so close. Their son was lost in guesswork and disbelief.

Grabbing her glass of amber liquid, Anne settled into the cushions of the sofa and took up the threads of her story.

A year after they met up in the *café des Ormes*, Mehmet sent Anne a message saying that he would be going through New York, and if there was any way she could get there, he would love to see her. Anne should probably have said no, but her curiosity prevailed. She had a lot of questions. What had happened to him after he found out about his link with Armenia? How had he put together, and accepted, this family puzzle that had changed so drastically? What would he do about his identity, which his grandmother had abruptly turned upside down? Difficult to find answers to any of these questions…

Making the trans-Atlantic flight, Anne went to stay with Arthur for a few days in the apartment where he still lived, on West 93rd Street in New York. They had been very close since they were children. But Mehmet's story had always been too painful for her to share with her brother. The episode of the Ottoman engagement and the marriage announcement that followed had left an open wound; at this point, it would be better to let sleeping dogs lie. Anne decided it best to hide the real reason for her visit. Arthur was happy about having his sister stay, but he tried to find out why she was coming for such a brief period of time. She told him she didn't want to be away from Joseph for too long, since he was still very young.

The day after she arrived, Anne met up with Mehmet while Arthur went off to college to teach his class. Mehmet was staying at the Plaza Hotel and invited Anne there, so she decided to walk through Central Park. She saw athletes of all ages. There were cyclists, runners and walkers, dressed in brightly colored outfits, sweating and out of breath. They seemed to take pleasure in their pain. It was an autumn day, mild yet cool at the same time. Anne had plenty of time to think on the long walk down there. She was very apprehensive, but couldn't put a finger on why.

The hotel was an imposing building on 5th Avenue. Standing outside in his formal livery, the concierge used a whistle to direct the taxis and limousines delivering guests to the building. Anne went into the entrance hall. It was so vast that you could have held a ball in the space. It was decorated with palm trees, whose leaves reached toward the glass panels above. The pink gladioli lovingly brushed up against the trees. A grand piano had been installed in a corner of the room. Its ivory keys glistened, and its lid was raised. It looked like a black panther in waiting, as if a concert were about to start. Photographs of famous guests were hung the length of one wall, smiles fixed in place on radiant faces, representing people who had honored the establishment with their presence over the years. This was a world of luxury and artifice. For a moment, Anne was tempted to turn back. She wondered why she had agreed to Mehmet's invitation. She went up to the welcome desk and spoke to a cordial yet irritatingly overeager employee. She explained that someone was expecting her. Once her presence was confirmed by a call to Mehmet, she was shown the way to the elevators. In the silence of the elevator on the way up, she wondered how her old fiancé had managed to stay in such a prestigious place. What was the reason for his visit to New York? Why had he wanted to see her?

She knocked on the door of Room 837, and Mehmet opened it immediately. He seemed impatient. He was pale, and he appeared to be even thinner than before. His frail figure stood in stark contrast with the décor of the room. In front of the bed, an imposing piece of furniture with sculpted legs, there were two armchairs covered in silk. The beige curtains were half drawn. A lamp with an imposing shade sat on a pedestal table, next to a basket of fruit that was so shiny that it seemed artificial. Anne went up to Mehmet and kissed him gently on the cheek. He had not shaved. Mehmet preempted Anne's questions. He told her that he was accompanying the Secretary of Health as official assistant, on a business trip, and that after a short stay in New York, he would continue to Washington.

Without any further ado, Mehmet want back to the revelation he had made in the *café des Ormes*. He told Anne that the story of his grandmother haunted him and would not leave him. His life was overshadowed by her sufferings. He admired her courage in facing her fate, and respected how she had kept her Armenian identity secret for decades. His grandmother must have deeply rejected the interior exile to which her executioners had condemned her. Two months prior, she had died at an advanced age, in silence and dignity. Now Mehmet felt that he was the guardian of her story. "I want to preserve her memory. She's part of me," he said, forcefully. And then added, "My grandmother's parents were killed, her name was taken away, and her life was stolen. I want to give it all back to her. It's time for vengeance." Anne listened on, horrified. With his newfound lack of restraint, her Ottoman fiancé had become a stranger. Despite her efforts, Mehmet would not back down. "You can't understand. It's me that has mixed blood, not you. My legacy is damned, not yours."

Suddenly, he jumped up, grabbed a bag next to the night table and approached Anne. He threw the bag down and pulled it open, feverishly emptying out its contents. "Wait, I'm going to show you...," he said. He never finished the sentence. Under a pile of carefully folded clothes, he took out a revolver and brandished it inside the hotel room as if it were a trophy. Anne was petrified. She looked at Mehmet and wondered if he had gone mad. She didn't know what to do. Mehmet laughed silently, and then, sadly, as if he had just made some great effort, he lowered his arm and threw the revolver on the bed. "Listen to me. I have a plan," he proclaimed in a decided tone that seemed out of place with his weary gestures. As Anne hunched up in the armchair, incapable of processing her shock, he added, "I've decided to kill the Secretary. I know that he's innocent, but he's going to pay for all the unpunished crimes, all those who escaped justice, those that committed the atrocities and then denied it. I am going to save the honor of my country." As he spoke, Anne saw a stream of saliva drip down his chin, and his lips quivered. Her blood ran cold. Mehmet was in another world, and no argument would bring him back. She gently put a hand on his arm, as if comforting a child. Then, paralyzed by fear, she got up, and left the room without saying a word.

When he got back to the apartment on 93rd Street that evening, Arthur found his sister stretched out on the sofa. Her hair was tousled and her swollen face bore traces of her trauma. Her brother was worried to see her like that and bombarded her with questions, which she avoided at first. But then, little by little, she recounted her visit to the room in the Plaza Hotel, and finally, her voice cracking, told Arthur about the revolver. He was incredulous and asked her if she was hallucinating. He was even more surprised by his sister's story because the subject of Mehmet had not even arisen since she broke off the engagement. Arthur did not know that they had remained in contact and had met in the *café des Ormes.* When Anne finished her story, he was beset by dark thoughts. What if Mehmet, in the grips of madness, had shot at her? After all, he seemed so worked up that the gun could have gone off at any moment. Unless it wasn't loaded, and Mehmet had just been exaggerating in front of Anne… it could have been anything. There was still the question of the police – should they warn the authorities that a potential killer was lurking in the opulence of this 5th Avenue hotel? Should they denounce Mehmet, or say nothing? Would they then become involuntary accomplices if Mehmet really did kill the secretary? They were so overwhelmed by this dilemma that they decided to wait until the following day to do anything.

They called a nearby restaurant and ordered some Italian food, which was delivered surprisingly fast. Hoping to lighten up such a dark evening, Arthur opened a richly colored bottle of wine. Brother and sister were happy to see each other again, strangely reunited under the wretched aura of Mehmet, the black angel casting a shadow over the room. To change the subject, Anne asked about Linda Wells, the neighbor with the yellow high-heeled shoes, whom Arthur had met when he moved to New York. He acted as though he was in love with her, although that hadn't stopped him from falling in love with other women at the same time… "She left," Arthur replied, relieved that they could talk about something more light-hearted. "Remember that she wanted to become a singer? Well, she's very determined, and she's going to do just that! She met a producer on the Internet. It was so lucky. Anyway, she moved to California and she's about to record her first pieces. Her grandfather was Polish, and she always promised herself that she would go back to her roots and take back their name. And so she did. Now, she's called Linda Kaczonowski."

After a short and restless night, Arthur got up first. He put on the coffee and was toasting some bread when Anne came out of the small bedroom. Tiredness in her eyes, she shuffled over to the bathroom. Then they sat down for breakfast. Once they had finished eating, Arthur got up and opened the front door, where the newspaper was waiting for him on the doorstep, just like every morning. He picked it up and scanned the first page, then cursed out loud. In capital letters, he read the headline: "MAN FOUND DEAD IN LUXURIOUS HOTEL ROOM." The article explained how the night before, at around 9 pm, Eva Méndez, an employee in a respected midtown establishment, was sent in to change the fruit basket laid out for the guests. She had knocked on the door of Room 837 and, on hearing no response, had gone into the room. A man was lying on the bed. She thought he was sleeping. She didn't want to disturb him, so she murmured some excuse and was about to leave when she noticed the red stains on the pillowcase. As she approached the man, she realized he was not breathing. She immediately informed a hotel representative, who alerted the managers. The information was succinct, but the paper explained that a guest at the hotel, a man in his thirties, had perished. It was the assistant of a Secretary visiting the country; however, the text explained, there was nothing to suggest that this was in any way related to politics. A doctor sent to the scene had confirmed the death as suicide, but since a foreign diplomat was involved, there was to be an additional investigation. The hotel management wanted to express its sincere condolences to the family and friends of the deceased. The report also added that, out of discretion for the family and in order not to interfere with police enquiries, no other details would be released to the press. In conclusion, the paper noted that, despite the questions they had posed to Eva Méndez, she was not authorized to reply.

Holding the paper in his hand, Arthur summarized the article. Anne seized on her brother's words. She went from a lack of comprehension ("But what's he talking about?") to disbelief ("It's not true, he's making it up!") until, eventually, she was overcome by grief. The day before, she had been presented with the opportunity to change the course of events… but she was powerless before this man in danger, and had left without a word. Once the door had closed, what anguish or madness had overcome Mehmet before he lay down, the revolver in his hand? She began to shake, and then to cry. As the tears poured down her face, Arthur took her in his arms. She sighed and rested her head on his shoulder. She tried to put her thoughts in order. The man who had put an end to his life in Room 837 was nothing like her old fiancé. She understood that Mehmet had crossed some boundary, and had entered into a world with no escape. He had become a prisoner of lies and secrets. They had enveloped him, trapped him, and finally smothered him in an evil cloak. He had killed himself. It was the only way out, his last recourse. Anne felt a great sadness, one that was mixed with a bitter and tender taste. She felt guilty that she had not managed to help or comfort Mehmet. These feelings were so difficult to admit. Arthur was the only one who had seen Anne's agony and could understand it. And from there on out, the brother and sister remained silent. The "great explanation" that Eric had demanded was the only thing that would eventually reveal the truth.

When Anne finished telling the story, Joseph went back quietly to his room, more upset than ever before. Behind Mehmet's story, behind his parents' story, there was a screen of blood and death. There had been men a century before, men who had decapitated people, raped women, massacred children. And then, a hundred years later, there was this pasty-faced character who had chosen (but was it really a choice, he wondered…?) to die alone in a New York hotel bed, an expiatory victim, killed by denial, trapped by a tragedy that he could not face.

Joseph sat on his bed. He covered his face with his hands. "I've heard enough. I think we have to put the past behind us. We descendants are like rabbits, trapped by a pack of poachers. Enough! I've had it. I know it's selfish, but that's how I feel. Armenia, my Armenia, I'm leaving you."

He took his phone out of his bag and looked for Clémence's number. He dialed it and she picked up. "Joseph, is that you?" she said, hesitantly. "I can't hear you properly. Your voice sounds strange…"

X

Amsterdam Avenue

Play it again, more slowly," Elmar Bruder ordered in his strong German accent. "You still haven't got it right. Your rhythm is off on the third bar, as I told you last week. And finish the phrase: *di-min-u-en-do*, you understand?" He dragged the syllables apart, gesturing with his hands, doubtless so as to reinforce his advice. When Elmar Bruder borrowed Joseph's cello to show him a difficult passage, this small man with drooping shoulders would disappear behind the instrument. Yet as he grabbed the bow and began to play, he underwent a metamorphosis. He drew himself up to his full height and with striking talent and authority, looked as though he were about to take off. In addition to his teaching, Elmar Bruder had a concert career. It took him all over the world and brought him in a tidy sum of money. His renown allowed him to select his own students, and he took advantage of this privilege with no scruples whatsoever. This made the other teachers jealous because it was a favor granted sparingly by the acclaimed conservatory in New York.

When Joseph applied to the program, he advanced through a merciless selection process until the final evaluation, when he had to play before the virtuoso. Elmar Bruder turned toward the window with a grouchy demeanor and thick-lipped pout. He seemed to be more interested in the traffic than in the effort of the young musicians, but he was actually listening very closely, although he didn't show it. Unlike his colleagues, Elmar Bruder did not assign any particular piece. Rather, he proclaimed in an eloquent tone, "The students present what they love to *me*, and in this way, I see what they are made of." Although his unorthodox approach was far from acceptable among the teachers, nobody dared to disagree. Immodest as he was, the man was untouchable. After the audition, he told Joseph tersely, "You've been accepted, Mr. Landolt. But I'm warning you, you've got a lot of work to do. It's going to be up to you." This comment was like a bucket of cold water thrown over the young man's enthusiasm. Joseph would have preferred to celebrate his success unreservedly. He told himself, "This teacher is hard. I'm going to struggle." His premonition would come true, even though he later found out that this was just the way his teacher was, oscillating between warning and threat.

To show "what he was made of," Joseph had chosen a Fauré sonata whose score he was very fond of. He was accompanied on the piano by a young Chinese woman who spoke so rarely that at first, he wondered if she was mute. He liked the piece he chose because it brought back happy memories of a family dinner. He had played the sonata in Kevork's honor one November evening. Aram's brother, who was staying in Geneva temporarily, was soon going back to Brazil. Having fled the dangers of the Amazon Forest, he had lived in the north of Rio for several years, operating a stall where he sold fresh produce, jams and American cigarettes. The store was barely adequate, but allowed him to make do. He regularly received financial assistance from Aram and Becca, even if he didn't ask for it. When he tried to thank them for the money, his brother and sister interrupted him. "It's nothing," they said. "You would do the same thing."

They had dinner in the house on the lake. There were stuffed vegetables that melted in your mouth, as well as lamb kebabs in a garlic sauce, eggplants and tomatoes. Between the main course and dessert, Joseph took out his cello and put the music on a stand because he didn't yet know Fauré's sonata by heart. He wanted to convince his family that, armed with his instrument ("my twin," as he called it), he was no longer an adolescent. Taking advanced courses in music was evidence of that. When he introduced the piece, there were admonitions and warnings. "That's a dangerous choice. You can't be sure it will work." Aram, in particular, was plagued by the anxiety that torments immigrants their entire lives, no matter how financially stable they become. "*Pasha* - the life of an artist?" he asked his grandson. "Are you sure you'll be able to earn a living? Music isn't guaranteed to feed you. Save the cello for a hobby. You won't run so many risks…" Yet Joseph smiled at every comment. He had made his choice, and his self-confidence was so strong that he could not be sidetracked.

When he played the last note, he felt his audience's approval ("Where did he get that gift?" they asked). And, understanding that he had won them over, he put down his bow and looked up. There in a corner of the room were his parents, silent and admiring, while Aram sat on the sofa at the other end of the room. Ever the patriarch and positioned in a place of authority, he had an arm around his sister Becca and his brother Kevork. The young musician looked emotionally at this trio marked by time, the tangle of wrinkles on their faces spelling out the difficulties of their lives. Age had left an especially strong imprint on Kevork, always the most fragile of the three, and at times his voice broke into a whisper. However, age had not destroyed their appetite. They devoured the honey cakes after the concert, picking up the leftover grains of sugar on the plate. Their hands shook lightly. Joseph imagined them as three sailors going back to port after a long voyage on rough seas. They looked ready to throw down the anchor and lower the flag. His intuition would be right. They would die one after the other in such a short time frame that it almost seemed they had agreed to do so. And with them, they took the world that they had known in the Ottoman Empire, a world whose rage and curse would never again be known.

The lesson was now over. The conservatory was a building of broken lines and unexpected angles, spectacularly transformed by an architect who specialized in glass and steel. In the corridors, Joseph repeated to himself the advice of his teacher, so that he would be sure to remember it. "You don't play with enough nuance, and your interpretation is too flat. For goodness' sake, remember that the movement finishes with a *diminuendo*." The young man was just leaving the school when he noticed something on the bulletin board. "My name's Elsie. I'm nine years old and I live on Amsterdam Avenue. I want to learn to play the cello, and I need to find a teacher who is <u>patient</u> (the word "patient" was underlined). Please reach me at 1 (212) 556-9594. Thank you. Elsie."

Joseph read the notice twice, intrigued by the child's writing, which looked immaculate. Elsie (or rather, no doubt, her family) was looking for a patient teacher, and this gave Joseph pause. He was a quick mover, and wasn't sure that he was all that tolerant, but he knew that patience was a necessary quality when you were teaching a musical instrument to a beginner, particularly a child. "That's interesting," he thought. "This young girl could be my first student. And I could use the money…" In the evening, he returned to his Uncle Arthur's apartment, where he was living until he found his own place. He picked up the phone and rang the number. Nobody answered at first, and he was about to hang up when he heard the voice of a young woman - at least, she sounded young. She spoke with a foreign accent that he could not place. "Well, why don't you come over? We can discuss it. Are you free tomorrow afternoon? We live on Amsterdam Avenue, on the corner of 89th Street, Apartment 15D." "And," she added, "Bring your cello."

That night, it snowed so heavily that at dawn, the city was spotless. An unusual silence seemed to cover everything, but that did not last. Soon, the snowplows began to move the snow into the gutters with a deafening noise. The clearing was underway, and continued until Joseph went to Amsterdam Avenue. He was carrying his cello, and had to take care not to slip on the frozen sidewalks. He was wearing a woolen jacket, but he had forgotten to put on a hat. When he arrived at the girl's house, he ran a hand through his hair. It was soaked, and in complete disarray, as usual. He was met by a doorman at the entry who looked stern, but sleepy. Joseph gave his name and said he was going to see Elsie. He was allowed up to the fifteenth floor. Stepping out of the elevator, he noticed a half-open door, and as he approached, a young woman appeared. She smiled, and greeted him. "Ah, here's the trio we were waiting for: the teacher, his cello, and the snow…. I was wondering if you would be able to come in this weather. Don't you have a hat? My name's Greta." "You must be Elsie's mother," Joseph guessed.

Greta shook her head, but did not offer any further explanation. She asked him if he would take off his wet shoes, and told him to come in. The apartment was huge and old-fashioned. "It was built in 1935," Greta explained. They walked down a dark corridor past several doors, and went into the living room. It was large and irregularly shaped, and led onto a balcony. The stacks of books and furniture was so impressive that at first, Joseph didn't notice a very elderly woman curled up on a velvet armchair. She was tiny, and looked like a squirrel that was about to be attacked by a bird of prey. The young man went up to her, but before he could say hello, he heard her exclaim in a clear, firm voice, quite out of keeping in such a frail body, "Look at that, you're in your socks! What a good idea, but your feet must be freezing cold, with this terrible weather. I see that you've met Greta.

She's going to make us some tea. I hope that you like black tea… It's the only kind we drink here." Without giving him a chance to react, or to introduce himself, she added, "I must warn you. Our tea is a little bitter. You might want to add some sugar. They say that sugar is an assassin that kills you slowly, but bitterness is also dangerous, especially if it takes hold of us surreptitiously. Don't you think?" As she said the word "surreptitiously," she separated each syllable carefully, and Joseph smiled. He thought about his cello teacher who spoke in the same way. The old woman sat up with difficulty, held out a hand that was gnarled by rheumatism, and in a tone that suddenly turned more formal, said, "Excuse me, I forgot to tell you my name. I'm Alma Klein. And this is Figaro." She pushed back the blanket covering her, and a Siamese cat appeared. He jumped from the old woman's knees to the ground and padded off.

She wanted to know if Joseph had had any difficulty finding the apartment, and as he reassured her, she said, "Do you know the origin of our address? Amsterdam Avenue is named after the first European colonists to New York. They were Dutch explorers who bought the island of Manhattan from the Indians, for a pittance. I used to teach history, and I've always been enthralled by New York. It's a cruel city, devoured by money. But it's also generous, and it welcomes you rather than rejecting you. You never get to know it completely, because it changes constantly… Sometimes, all it takes is a night for entire buildings to be destroyed. Rats come out of the rubble and disappear into the subway. Then you look up and see a new building, taller and even more luxurious! And New York has beautiful museums. Do you like museums?" Without waiting for a reply, Alma Klein asked Joseph if he would play something for her. He was a little taken aback, but agreed to do so, so he leaned over, took out his cello, tuned it, and announced, as if he were in a concert hall, "Bach, suite No. 1."

He was just finishing the prelude when he noticed that Alma Klein had closed her eyes and seemed to be asleep. Hesitating, he wondered if he should continue. But right at that moment, Greta came back in, a tray in her hand. She poured the tea into small china cups, and said, "I liked hearing you play. Don't think that Mrs. Klein is getting bored. Far from it, even if she drops off easily. She's an expert at taking catnaps! You know, she'll be 87 next month."

"I understand. I imagine that she's Elsie's grandmother…"

"No, not really," Greta said, stroking the cat, who walked in front of her.

After a moment's silence, she added,

"Don't forget to put sugar in your tea or it will really be too bitter. I suppose you would like to meet your student."

"Of course, I would be delighted. Hasn't she arrived yet?"

"No, I'm sorry, she isn't here. She was supposed to be coming back from school, but she missed her train. We should have told you, I know, but Alma was so anxious to meet you…"

"Me too. I was excited about coming here, also. It's my very first lesson."

"Oh really? So, you've never taught?"

"No, I'm still a student. And what about you?" asked Joseph, turning toward the young woman. "Have you lived here long?"

"I'm Mrs. Klein's assistant, though I also cook sometimes," she added, smiling. She had beautiful dark eyes. Joseph thought that she was very pretty. "I come in the morning, help Alma get dressed, and have breakfast with her. Then we sit in the study. A few years ago, before she stopped teaching at the university, the very idea of retirement was unthinkable. She wouldn't even allow you to mention the 'R' word! She didn't want to stop working, so she has continued doing her research. I help her organize her documents and take care of her mail. She gets loads of letters, and requests, too. She's very well known. She's even been on prime-time TV. You should have seen her! She was a real hit because she knows how to present difficult topics in language that's easy to understand. Look at these books she wrote on the Second World War."

Greta showed him two thick texts on a shelf, and Joseph leafed through them before continuing,

"And Mrs. Klein loves New York, if I understood her rightly…"

"She goes on and on about it. She always says she's in love with it. Sometimes she says, 'Enough books and paperwork! Let's go out.' Then we stop everything. She puts on her black cloak, and out we go. We walk slowly through the streets in the neighborhood, as if we're discovering the charm of New York for the first time. She loves everything - the bright lights, the rumbling of the subway, the pizza delivery people on their bikes, the dog walkers with all those dogs on leashes… You should hear the way she laughs and talks! She's right, you know…"

"Was she born here?"

"No. She was born in Germany before the war, to a Jewish family. She lived in Frankfurt and her father was a doctor. His father and grandfather had been doctors before him, in the same office. But they didn't see the warning signs and came close to losing their lives. As the months passed and there were more threats, they ignored them. For a long time, it seemed impossible, even absurd, that the country where they and their ancestors were born could reject them. Even today, Alma remembers a comment they used to make at the dinner table, so ludicrous if you think about it: 'Nothing can happen to us in the country of Goethe and Mendelssohn…' Her parents were blind, in denial. In

1938, at the very end, they finally realized they needed to leave, and they fled the country. They found an undercover rescuer, paid him a fortune, and escaped to Portugal. From Lisbon, they took a ship that brought them here. They just managed to avoid the catastrophe."

"… so for them, New York was a kind of refuge," Joseph said.

"Yes, that's it. After that, Mrs. Klein never wanted to leave the city and has always refused assignments that were offered to her elsewhere, even prestigious ones. Quite logical, actually."

"And you, Greta? Where do you come from?"

"What makes you think I'm not from here?"

"You have a slight accent, but I can't place it."

"I'm glad it's slight, because I would like to lose it. I bet that even if you tried, you could never guess!"

"Is that a challenge?" he asked, laughing. "OK, I accept."

"No, no. I have a rare accent, that's all."

"I'm curious. Wait, if you give me a hint, I can definitely guess. Help me!"

"No way!" Greta exclaimed before changing her mind. "OK, fine, seeing as you're so nice, I'll give you a clue, but only one! It's a city in the Caucasian mountains. The capital of a small country…"

"Yerevan, the capital of Armenia," Joseph said, surprised by the coincidence. "I won the bet, right?" ("But I won't get a prize," he wanted to add.)

"Bingo! How did you know? Not many people know about Yerevan. I can't believe…"

"I've always liked geography," Joseph interrupted. He had no wish to tell her the troubled story of his family. He asked Greta if she took care of Elsie.

"No, not really. She goes to boarding school during the week. She only comes back here on weekends."

"Isn't Elsie in her room?" Alma Klein said, waking up. "She must be reading, as usual. Greta, could you tell her that this young man is here to give her a lesson? She shouldn't make him wait."

There was a moment of silence.

"You forgot. Elsie missed her train. She stayed at school."

"That's really a nuisance. I'm going to call the principal and complain. They don't watch over the students enough. They always leave them to their own devices. I'm sure she would have caught the train if she'd been reminded to hurry up. I mean, she's only nine… I'm so sorry for this inconvenience, Mr. Joseph."

The young man, in stockinged feet and with his hair, now dry but still tousled, found it weird to be called "Mr. Joseph." But he smiled, and said nothing. He was sitting on the sofa next to Greta, their knees barely touching. Figaro was under a low table, scratching at the embroidered roses that adorned the expensive rug. Joseph noticed a framed photo in the middle of the library. He was able to make out a faded, old-fashioned image of Alma Klein, a shadow cast over her face by her straw hat. Beside her was a young girl in a summer dress, looking straight ahead. She was carrying a bucket in her left hand, and her feet were covered with sand. At the edge of the photo, a little further back, there was a yellow parasol in front of a house with closed shutters. In the distance, there was a young man, who appeared to be looking at Alma Klein and the child. "It looks like a Hopper painting," Joseph thought. Three people, together and yet separate. They are out of focus, yet each has a strong presence. The yellow parasol, the house and the man in the background are partly cut off. Perhaps the photographer didn't want to capture the entire scene, and let the viewers fill it out with their imagination…"

Joseph was about to get up and say goodbye when Alma Klein asked him to play some more. He chose *The Swan*, the piece that he had played at his grandfather's funeral.

"Magnificent," Alma Klein said when he finished. "I would love Elsie to learn to play that piece! We'll see you next week, Mr. Joseph, and I promise that your student will be on time."

Greta took Joseph to the door. They said goodbye, and he headed for the elevator.

"So, snowman," Arthur asked his nephew when Joseph got back to the apartment on West 93rd Street, numb with cold. "How was the lesson? Did you find your calling in life?"

"Nope! No calling in life, and no student!"

"What do you mean? You went there for nothing? You must be joking."

"Let me tell you what happened. Imagine a huge apartment stacked full of books and old furniture. I was met by a very old woman and her assistant. And Figaro, a Siamese cat."

"Oh, I see, so it's the cat who wants to study cello! But no girl? So you're telling me you wasted your time?"

"Not really. I had some tea, and Greta…"

"Greta?"

"Yes, the young woman who takes care of Mrs. Klein."

In a few sentences, Joseph described Greta, her accent, and the role she played in the apartment on Amsterdam Avenue. "She's pretty and she's nice. I really like her."

"Oh là là, so you've met someone!" Arthur exclaimed, tapping on the boy's shoulder. (He knew that after a few years, Joseph's relationship with Clémence Dumas had ended.)

"You'll never believe this. She's from Armenia."

"That's perfect! What did she say when you told her about yourself?"

"Well, nothing," Joseph answered tersely. Arthur was astonished.

"What? Didn't you tell her?"

"No, I didn't want to roll out our autobiography. It wasn't the moment, and anyway, we need to tear ourselves away from that terrible story. We were born in Geneva, and now we are in the United States… far away from it all."

"And your roots, are you going to forget them? Refuse to acknowledge them?"

Joseph didn't answer the question. He couldn't find words to express his feelings. It was difficult and painful, even impossible, to explain both the throes of emotion that had plagued him since childhood, and their seismic impact on his spirit and his heart. He was a mass of contradictions. Armenia embodied pride and sadness, victims and fighters, an open cemetery. But at the same time, it was the seat of renewal. His family's silence about the past (it was a taboo subject, even though nobody ever said it) had left Joseph alone with questions, doubts, and sometimes, even surprises. He had not forgotten that just before his death, his *papig* Aram had encouraged him to learn the language of his ancestors and to discover their literature. That was in vain. Joseph never followed up on it, even though he was dearly attached to his grandfather, who had always represented a safe haven. Joseph moved even further from his roots when he learned about what had happened to Mehmet, up to and including his suicide in the Plaza Hotel. He was so upset by this event that he felt like he had slipped down a mountain. He had dropped the rope that held him to his past.

"When I found out about Mehmet's death, I…"

"How do you know about that?" Arthur asked. "Did your

mom tell you? I didn't think she ever wanted to talk about it again."

"Yeah, but one evening, my father was so insistent that she told him the entire saga. They were drinking whiskey, and she let out the whole thing…"

"In front of you?" asked Arthur, incredulously.

"No, not really. I heard them talking, but she doesn't know that. I was hiding in the corridor."

"What? You were spying on them?"

Joseph admitted it. His curiosity had gotten the better of him, and he really wanted to know what everyone had been concealing from him.

"I needed to know, to reconstruct the puzzle. You can understand that, right?"

"Wait, don't go down that road. Just tell yourself that Mehmet lost his head. At this point, we have nothing to do with him."

"That's not exactly true. We could have met the same end, and that scares me. We should talk about something else."

"You know, when I was your age, I thought like you…"

"And did you change your mind, *my old man*?" Joseph asked, laughing. (He liked reminding Arthur that time had passed, even if his blue-eyed uncle still thought himself young and attractive, taking care of his body, avoiding greasy food and making sure to go to the gym.)

"That's right, I changed my mind. When I got to New York, I wanted to begin again, pull up my roots and start from scratch. We all love each other in the family, but I wanted to try something different. Become a new man, you see? I'd heard enough about the drama with my sister and her Ottoman fiancé, plus it had become hard to bear the pressure my parents were putting on me to find a career and make some money. It was only later that I finally got it. You can't bury the past so easily."

"And yet you stayed in the United States and didn't have any children? Did you want to break the family lineage or something?"

"Maybe, actually. I don't know. But there's still time, buddy," Arthur said, looking at his nephew with a smile of amusement. I could still have a child. And in that case, you would not be the sole inheritor of the dynasty! What do you say about that?"

"Ha ha. No problem! I'd be very happy. It's hard to be the only one carrying the torch…"

Arthur got up, declaring, "OK, enough deep thinking for today. It's dinner time. Let's make something simple… a ham omelette and some tomatoes on the side? Will that be enough?"

"Perfect! I'm starving."

Once they had eaten and washed the dishes, Joseph took out his cello. Even though he had practiced the difficult sections in Fauré's sonata, it still gave him trouble. The more he tried to correct his mistakes, the worse he did. He'd been studying the piece for a long time, but nothing seemed to go right. When the rhythm was finally in place, his interpretation felt unwieldy, and he became discouraged. The delicate nature of the music had disappeared. He wanted to tear up the score and knock over the stand. He could already hear Elmar Bruder in his ear. He would definitely be angry, and remind him that there were still other pieces, even more challenging, that he needed to move on to.

Joseph also thought about his parents. They had agreed to pay for his studies, which were expensive, and he might need to concede that he had failed. Perhaps the truth was that he would never become the musician he had dreamed of becoming. It was just a pipe dream. He should give it up and return the instrument to its case. He put down the bow, and for a second, imagined a world without music. But that was impossible. Instead of throwing in the towel, he should get back up and fight. He picked up the cello, and forced himself to play the piece over, tackling the bars that he had been avoiding. "That's better," he said to himself. "Again. Let me get back to it." He did not stop practicing until two hours later, and he looked out the window. The snow was still falling. He closed his eyes, overcome by fatigue. Gabriel Fauré came into the room, some sheet music in his hand. "It's time to wake up, Joseph," he said. "Last night, I composed something for you. You'll be the first one to play it."

The following week, the weather improved. The piles of muddy snow had melted and turned into black puddles. When Joseph got to the building on Amsterdam Avenue, the doorman was not at his desk, so he went straight up to the fifteenth floor and rang the buzzer to 15D. Greta took a long time to answer, and when she did, she looked very upset. She motioned him to come in, and they went into the living room. It was empty.

"What's the matter?" Joseph asked.

"Alma… she died last night."

"What? So suddenly? What happened?"

"Around five o'clock, we had something light to eat – some fruit and some cookies. Then, she started reading the paper, just like she always did, and dozed off. When I went up to her, I noticed that she had slid down into the armchair. I wanted to help her sit up, but she was very heavy even though she is" (Greta used the present tense) "so slender. She was breathing in fits and starts, so I called the doctor, but he didn't answer. Then I called Emergency. They sent an ambulance right away, but it was too late."

"I don't know what to say. I'm so sorry… And did you

tell Elsie?"

"No, that's impossible."

"Impossible? Why?"

Greta pushed Joseph toward the book shelves and showed him the faded photograph in the middle of the books.

"Do you recognize Alma?" she asked.

"Yes, of course, even though her face is partly hidden by her hat."

"And do you see the girl next to her? That's her daughter. Elsie."

"I'm sorry, I'm not following you. Are you saying that Elsie is Mrs. Klein's daughter?"

"That's right. Alma had a daughter, Elsie. She died fifty years ago."

Joseph looked so taken aback that Greta could not stifle a smile.

"Look, you deserve an explanation. I'm going to tell you the story behind that photograph. That summer, Alma was on vacation in Maine, in New England, with her husband (the man in the background) and their daughter. They loved that region, and they spent every July there in a wooden house on the beach. One afternoon, Alma was busy working on a book, so Robert Klein decided to rent a rowboat and take Elsie out. The weather was beautiful. But suddenly, the sun went in and dark clouds came up over the horizon. There can be unexpected thunderstorms in that area, along with violent winds and huge waves. And that's what happened. The coast guards sent out distress flares and immediately deployed the rescue boats, but it was no use. The father and daughter disappeared. They were never seen again."

"And Alma?"

"When she learned that Robert and Elsie had drowned, she threw herself into her work. Night and day. She would never leave it. She read, wrote, published, and taught. She barricaded herself into her office, and refused to speak to anyone, even her best friends. You know, she may be frail, but she is a force of nature" (again, Greta used the present tense). "And intimidating. Nobody could help her or console her."

"As if she had put her pain to rest…"

"Exactly, but you know that if you are in so much pain, it can't be ignored. It comes back, even after a long time. You can't bury it forever. Alma remained brilliant, but little by little, she started to lose her mind."

Greta told Joseph how Elsie had slowly begun to come back to life after having been swept away by the waves fifty years before. At first, she was just an outline, a shadow puppet, and then she began to take shape. Alma Klein saw her, called her, and read aloud to her. The elderly woman became consumed by her imagination, which grew bigger day by day.

"And didn't you tell her?" Joseph asked.

"At first, I tried to make her remember the storm and the disaster, but she wouldn't believe me. She told me that luckily, Robert was a great sailor and he'd managed to get the boat back safely. When I said, 'Mrs. Klein, you're wrong, you know that Elsie and her father never came back,' she would give me a blank look, as if she didn't get it."

Slowly, current circumstances started to escape Alma. She took refuge in her memories, and after a while, Greta gave up and joined her. It was an astonishing journey. They entered another world together. "No doubt I should have called the doctors to inform them of this… madness" (it was difficult for Greta to say the word), "but I didn't dare. I worried that Alma would be sent to an institution. I understood that she could no longer bear reality, so I helped her to dream the rest of her life away. Of course, you might try to guilt trip me, even condemn me, but too bad. I can live with that."

Joseph's mind was flooded with questions he was unable to answer. What would he have done in that situation? Was it right to drift off with that woman, or to stand up in the name of lucidity and a truth that was too heavy to bear? Had Greta been an unconscious, even dangerous accomplice, or an infinitely well-meaning friend? Perhaps the wisest course of action was to avoid judging her. For once, it was better to stay away from the comfortable, reassuring categories of true and false, good and bad. This story of impossible love and loss affected Joseph deeply. As if she could see his thoughts, Greta said,

"You must find this all strange, but it was stronger than me. I couldn't resist. I had to indulge her…"

"And Alma's family?"

"The only one left is a cousin. She lives in California and I don't know her. Soon, I'll call to tell her that Mrs. Klein has passed away."

Greta put her hand on Joseph's arm.

"I hope you're not mad at me. I should have told you that there wouldn't be any cello lessons."

At that moment, the Siamese cat sauntered majestically into the room, rounding his back and rubbing against Joseph's legs.

"And Figaro? What will happen to him?" Joseph asked.

"I'll take him with me. I live in Brooklyn. You can come and visit him," Greta suggested. "He would be glad to see you."

"Of course. I'd love to. In the meantime, why don't we have some tea?"

"Good idea. You mustn't forget the sugar - this tea is bitter," Greta reminded him. She went over to the kitchen.

Harry Koumrouyan

XI

The Actor in the Orange Sweater

The room was flooded in golden sunlight. It was a few months later, a Sunday morning in Brooklyn. At that time of day, the street was calm, almost provincial. Manhattan seemed a long way off, although it was easy to get to. You could just take a short trip on the subway, or walk across one of the bridges into the city. You could see the broken line of tall buildings through the cables and arches of the walkway. There was a light breeze from the ocean and the river. In the distance, her arm raised triumphantly, the Statue of Liberty guarded the port of New York.

Figaro jumped on the bed, stretched, and then, with great pleasure, slid for a moment of peace between the sleeping bodies. He pawed Joseph's shoulder insistently, and then turned toward Greta to nuzzle up against her cheek where the pillowcase had left wrinkles on her skin. "It's too early," Joseph grumbled, and he disappeared under the sheets, hoping to go back to sleep. Greta did not move. Perhaps this would dissuade the cat from waking them up entirely. Nice try: the game was up. Breakfast time had come and gone, and Figaro, half cuddly toy and half cat, decided that it was time for them to take care of him. No indolent morning in bed, as tender as it may be, could justify this delay. There was no use fighting against this pet, who considered himself a landlord, timekeeper and organizer of every festive moment. Thrown off the bed by an angry arm, he skidded on the beautiful cherry wood floor, and jumped right back up to the lazy people in the bed. If banished to the living room, he would meow behind the closed door until they got tired of arguing with him and agreed to prepare his milk and cookies.

Outside, some teenagers were yelling loudly to each other. "Hey, Tony, go get the ball. Hurry up! We'll wait for

185

you in the playground." Tony was Mrs. Rodríguez's son and he lived on the first floor. He cursed in reply. His squeaky voice, which had not yet dropped, was drowned out by the sound of a truck. There was a screech of brakes under the windows. Joseph reached out a hand and sent a pillow flying the floor. "OK, I understand," he said, sleepily. "I'll have to sleep in another day." He looked at Greta, who had pushed the covers aside, and smiled as he saw her naked breast. "She's so pretty," he thought, and leaned toward her warm body. He took her into his arms, but Figaro would not give up. He knew that his goal was in sight. "You're such a pain in the neck, buddy," Joseph muttered, getting out of bed. "If you carry on like this, I'll throw you outside." The cat protested and winked, as if he got the idea. Greta gently intervened, "Oh no, you won't. We'll take care of you, Figaro. You have nothing to fear from this guy."

Joseph went to the kitchen, followed by Figaro, who made a beeline to his bowl. The cat watched, resolutely, and plunged his face into the milk as soon as it was poured, savoring his victory. Joseph put the coffee on, poured some orange juice into glasses and added a little leftover champagne that he found in the refrigerator. He took a tray from the cabinet and put the cups and glasses onto it. The coffeepot hissed in its familiar way, and Joseph ran over the past few weeks in his mind. After Alma Klein's death, her cousin from California had come to the apartment on Amsterdam Avenue. She was a heavy-set blond woman of about fifty years old, with crooked teeth. "We have to empty the place in a week," she warned them, "so we've got no time to lose, and no time for sentimentality. I'm going to take some furniture" (she chose the beautiful writing desk in the hall); "you take the rest if you want. Otherwise, I'll call the movers to get rid of everything. Oh, and do you think we should give Alma's books and papers to the university? Well, why not, if they're interested? Frankly, it makes no difference to me. Do whatever you want." Since Greta's apartment in Brooklyn was already cramped, she only kept a few small things. She asked Alma's cousin if she could keep the photograph in the middle of the bookcase. "No problem. Are you sure you want it? The colors are so faded that you can't see a thing… You can just make out Alma, but who's that young girl?" Greta didn't respond. She slipped the photo carefully into her bag. The cousin was surprised at how much care she took, and laughed, "My word, you'd think that you were taking something valuable!" That same evening, Greta felt very lonely, and without thinking too much, she called Joseph, who was happy to hear her voice. They saw each other the following day, and then again and again. When they made love for the first time, it was both tender and wild, as these long-awaited moments can be. Some weeks later, Joseph took his cello and his belongings (not much, in fact; two or three books, his sheet music, some linen and a coat that his parents had bought him for his birthday) and moved in with Greta. When he told Arthur about his move, his uncle exclaimed: "Ha, look at my nephew! It's getting serious. You should talk to Ms. Brooklyn about your connection with Armenia. It's kind of weird to keep it secret, don't you think?"

Joseph was thinking the exact same thing as he put the tray of drinks down on the bed.

"Coffee and orange juice!" Greta said. "Fantastic. Figaro did a good thing by waking us up."

"Yeah, right. I could easily have slept another hour. But I suppose we'll console ourselves with a little champagne. It's gone flat, but whatever."

Joseph picked up the pillow and sat on the bed. He grabbed a glass, raised it, and looked at Greta.

"I've got something to tell you," he announced, sounding more solemn than he intended.

"You're acting very serious," Greta said, smiling. "I thought you'd already told me everything."

"Not really. I was scared of moving too fast. In music, you learn to control the tempo, and it's the same in life."

"Wait, now you're scaring *me*. Keep your secrets, if you want! You know, lovers don't have to tell each other everything."

"That's true. But still, I need to tell you something."

"OK. You're an honest guy, so if you need to confess, feel free. For example, if you cheated on the girl that loves you, or if you have been in jail for armed robbery, or if…"

"No, you're way off," Joseph interrupted. "It's much simpler than all that: well, I hope so…"

"Go on, I'm listening," Greta said. She placed her hands on the sheets, acting as though she were serious.

But Joseph said nothing. "Perhaps I shouldn't continue," he thought to himself. But then he dove right in.

"I…"

He stopped.

"Yes?"

"Greta, there are two Armenians in this bed."

"What? You must be kidding! Joseph Landolt, my boyfriend, is Armenian? What next?"

"You'll understand everything when I tell you my mother's name…"

"Wait, it's Anne, right?"

"Well, not really. She changed her name."

"What was it before?"

"Anoush. She was 'Anoush Simonian' when she was born, then she became 'Anne,' and when she got married, 'Anne Landolt.' You're going to think this is weird, but in the diaspora, and especially in my family, we sometimes want to forget our roots, no matter how proud we are of them."

"Why would you want to forget them? What for? Your

mother changed her name? That's not the kind of thing people do! Why didn't you tell me, Joseph? You were lying to me." Greta sounded angry, speaking faster and faster.

"I didn't lie to you. I just didn't tell you. That's not the same thing."

"Lying by omission is a form of not telling the truth. What were you afraid of?"

"Nothing, I'm telling you."

"Oh no? Then it's even worse. You were ashamed. You wanted to hide things from me. Like camouflage. At your concert, they'll say, 'Ladies and Gentlemen, we're pleased to introduce a promising cellist, Joseph Landolt, who was born in Geneva, and studies in New York.' Obviously, that sounds better than 'Joseph Simonian, who moved from Yerevan to Brooklyn with a hundred dollars in his pocket.'"

Joseph was disheartened. What did he do wrong? Just because he had a comfortable family, who were well established in their new life? Was it the weak link with the past? The fact that he didn't speak his ancestors' language? Or maybe all of the above. He got up and pushed back the sheets.

"What are you blaming me for?" he asked sharply. "What did I do wrong? Come on, read me a list. I'm all ears. Maybe I should give you some excuses…"

"Just stop this circus. I'm upset how you can break ties with Armenia like that. As if it's just a bad memory or something. It's gross, you know. And it's very hurtful."

"You're not being fair, Greta, and it's not based on anything. Plus, you're in no place to judge me. After all, you yourself left Armenia…"

"And I'm sure you know why. I didn't choose to leave. It was poverty that pushed me out. A forced exile. You really don't understand a thing, do you?"

Greta got out of bed. She paced furiously up and down the room, and then went to the bathroom. She ran the water, yanked a drawer open and slammed it shut. A few minutes later, she came back into the bedroom, put on her jacket and grabbed her bag. Without a word, she went out, tugging on the door so hard that the building shook. Joseph was alone. He was disoriented, as if he'd just received a blow to the head and was seeing stars. He fought to put his ideas in order, but there was no way. He was despondent for a long time, but then he picked up his blue notebook and began to write, picking up speed as he went along.

Greta kicked up a fuss. Screw her. (Then he took this out.) *What's her problem with me, anyway? No identity... A historical blur? I didn't say anything. She wanted me to be the standard bearer. Chin up and long live Armenia, etc. Of course, I was handed the flag, but I was under no obligation to wave it around, right? Greta thinks (or is afraid) that I'm going to put it in the vault and get it out one day when it's all dusty and full of holes. Maybe she's right, and that's the risk I'm taking. But we don't share the same story, me and her. We're not from the same place, and we haven't been through the same things. I was born in Europe, not in Yerevan. And so what? Is that a problem? If I don't flaunt my origins, I've become a traitor to my country, a privileged Westerner who has left his compatriots in the lurch* (he changed the last words to "in misery," which sounded more noble) *and is now living a beautiful life somewhere else.*

Greta and I are different, and that's why I'm attracted to her. She should understand that. Back in the day, maybe our grandparents were neighbors, or cousins, or lovers! You never know, and we'll never know, and we have to live with that. There is no genealogy, there are no archives, there are no old photos. The genocide took everything away, people and their things. You can't turn back the clock. This film was shredded apart and it ended shakily. And I'm not the scriptwriter or even an actor. Maybe I'm just an extra. Well, OK, I might be a coward, but I just don't want to go back in time on a guilt trip. I'm not a militant for anybody's cause. Am I being selfish or lazy? Or do I lack courage? Let's see. I was born after the massacres, and I didn't experience fear or bloodshed. It's true that I've been lucky until now. What do I owe that to? Who is the great organizer? God, destiny, chance, or simply, like in children's tales, the nice little fairy leaning over the crib? I don't know. And actually, I couldn't care less. Well, not completely... I'm still not sure.

All of a sudden, a fireball darted across the room. It was Figaro. He had lost his footing, and looked thwarted. The insect he was chasing had gotten away. Joseph offered him some salmon. The cat listened carefully as he recovered from his fall. He understood the hint, and began to purr. On the first floor, Mrs. Rodríguez opened the window and shouted out to Tony, "Hurry up! Dinner's ready, and we're waiting for you!"

Yervant Manoukian was alone on the stage in his bright orange sweater, pleated chinos and high-top sneakers. The show, titled *About-Face*, took place every evening at 7 p.m. in a brick building in Red Hook, a neighborhood on the Brooklyn seafront. The coffeehouse-theater was tiny, but it had a devoted fan base. It was oddly located on the third floor of the building, in what used to be a shoe factory. You reached the room via a freight elevator, which was so slow that some of the spectators preferred the fire escape. Up until then, the actor, who was about thirty or so, was little known.

He had some minor roles in a police series, obtained, he regretfully thought, more for his Armenian appearance (very dark hair, average height, deep-set eyes) than for his talent. He feared that he would be typecast, and would have liked to take on a wider range of parts. On top of that, he was the stand-in for a Broadway star whose name was emblazoned in gold letters on the front of the theater. Although this famous actor led a passionate life even in his dressing room, surrounded by illicit products and loose women, he appeared to possess an iron constitution. Yervant, the silent understudy, was forever confined to the backstage. He was obliged to be present at the shows, ready to assume the title role if, by chance, the actor did not show up at the last minute. Unfortunately, this was never meant to happen.

Although resolutely optimistic by nature, Yervant began to doubt that he would ever be able to find a place, even a small one, in the galaxy of New York theater. He was beset by despondency. "I'm a stranger, an impostor. They'll get rid of me." He thought of giving up acting. "The stage, the spotlights… I'll save that for another life." But overnight, things suddenly took a better turn. His career took off - proof that there is a God, and that sometimes he takes care of penniless actors. His show was written up unexpectedly: "Check out this great young actor in a Brooklyn theater." Then he was interviewed on the radio, where he charmed the host with his lively comebacks and sense of humor. Word of mouth did the rest, and in a few weeks, he was riding the wave so high that it became difficult to get seats at his show. To the great surprise of his agent, who thought Yervant was a nice guy but not necessarily a future star, the theater manager decided to put on some extra performances.

Some time before, Joseph and Greta had read about the actor in the paper and bought tickets. They were still annoyed with each other, but met up in the theater on the Friday after their argument. Neither of them tried to give any excuses or explanations. Greta still wondered why Joseph had hidden his family's history from her for so many months, while Joseph could not understand why she had gotten so angry once she learned the truth. Only Figaro, always happy to see them, tried to make amends. He went from one to the other, as if he hoped that under the circumstances, he could play the role of benevolent ambassador.

The show began. Yervant was alone on the set, standing in an imaginary kitchen and talking to his mother, who he also played, blithely splitting his performance into two roles. The mother, headscarf on her head, was making meatballs. She was about to disappear when her dear son, the oldest of the siblings and the object of her constant attentions, announced that he was going to emigrate. "No," she cried. "You can't. When I die, you won't be there to close my eyes." Then she started to cry. "Too bad. Just go, and leave me alone." Finally, her voice getting louder and louder, she became more aggressive. "Leave now. I'm going to call the neighbor, Noubar. He's a kind man, and he'll take care of me." The audience was swept away by the story of this mother and her son. It was unique and distinctive, yet at the same time universal. Both the harsh and the funny parts had touches of tenderness, used sparingly, with a mixture of laughter and emotion. The actor could do everything: speak, sing, and juggle with words and with his body. He had an astonishing presence, strong and yet reserved, personifying power and reticence. Despite the restricted space of the set, he managed to move around constantly. He would approach the audience, and just as he was running out of space, turn back, sometimes even disappearing in the wings. A moment later, he would emerge once more, leaping around as if he were on a pogo stick. He bounced back and forth so much that the audience had trouble following him. The transitions between different episodes were marked by a jazz melody on a double bass.

After a brief intermission, the artist came back on stage, carrying a beaten-up suitcase. It was his only prop, and it magically transformed into symbol after symbol. First, it represented the voyage (despite his mother's pleading, Yervant decided to leave Armenia), then it was the plane landing at Kennedy Airport (a tragic yet hilarious scene pitting the young man and his dubious English against an immigration agent who bombarded him with a barrage of questions, while at the same time demanding that the dazed passenger get his fingerprints taken), and finally it stood in for the apartment in Brooklyn (a shoebox that the character shared with some surprising friends: a poet with translucent skin, besotted with yoga, a Belgian fashion designer who created low-neck dresses while languishing on his bed, and a marathon runner, who got up at dawn and ran bare-chested through the park nearby, his gaze fixed on his stopwatch).

The play was drawing to a close when suddenly, a member of the audience got up from her chair in the third row and started to heap abuse on the actor. "Hey, are you trying to make this story about you? Are you loading your experiences off on us, or is this make-believe?" The other members of the audience were angered by this outburst, and after a few seconds of shock, asked her to sit down and shut up. A round-shouldered older man sitting next to her whispered, "You're being very rude. You're upsetting everyone." One of the workers in the theater, a technician no doubt, went up to her and gestured for her to stop making so much fuss. At first, she looked straight ahead and seemed to calm down, but after a moment's respite, she turned agitated once more. She ignored the indignant comments of the audience and started up again. "So, Yervant, you had a hard time getting here? What, do you miss your own country?"

Yervant did not lose his composure. In response to her last comments, he made up a verse on the spot. "I had some trouble getting here; my country is there, my country is here." He bent his knees and held out his hands, slipping the title of the show, *About-Face*, into the song. Then, to the great surprise of the audience, he went up to the woman in the third row, took her by the hand, and invited her up to the stage. At that moment, the double bass began to play, the volume rising. They began to dance before the astounded crowd. The woman took him in her arms, caressed his neck, and clasped him closely to her, as if preparing to smother him. He pulled away and carried on singing. "Don't box me in: I am from here; I am from there. Don't box me in…" Specks of silver glitter unexpectedly fell from the loft, creating a shower of light.

The curtain fell. Yervant Manoukian came out to greet the audience, together with his accomplice. She gave a playful smile, and there were enthusiastic cries of "Bravo!" The elderly man who had spoken out stood up, and soon the whole audience was on their feet, applauding. The actor bowed, drops of perspiration on his face. His shoes were untied. He showed no sign of fatigue, visibly pleased to have played his roles so intensely and satisfied with the mood he had created.

Joseph and Greta really liked the show, and decided to wait for the actor at the exit. When he appeared a quarter of an hour later, his makeup had been removed and he was carrying a bottle of water in his hand. They asked him to sign the program, and he was happy to comply. Then, he looked up. For no apparent reason, he said, "Hey, you two, keep your spirits up!" No other words passed between them. Yervant went off, light-hearted and happy. His orange suit shone in the night.

When Joseph and Greta got to the apartment, they heard Figaro meow. He was waiting for them behind the door. They fed him, and sat in the living room. The magic of the show was still in the air around them. Unprompted, Joseph began to tell Greta the story of his family: how Aram, Kevork and Becca had fled, chased out by the Ottomans through the Sublime Porte. He went into particular detail on their experiences in Geneva and Brazil, and told her about the vacuum everyone felt after their death. He spoke of his parents, their indestructible bond that remained in spite of their disagreements, the mysterious chemistry that brought them together and separated them. He mentioned Mehmet, his sinister project and his tragic death in a hotel in New York. He described his Uncle Arthur with the blue eyes, his brief career as an actor, and the fact that he didn't have any children. Joseph spoke as never before. His voice serious in tone, he disclosed episodes of the torn and indistinct novel of his life. When he finished his story, late into the night, Greta was very moved.

"And what about you, in all this?" she asked.

Joseph replied with no hesitation,

"I have my cello, you know."

"And before? When you were small?

"I used to hide behind the curtains in the living room, but Lolo would always find me. She made me the best rice pudding in the world… I can still remember it."

There was a moment of silence. They looked at each other as if for the first time. Joseph put his hands on Greta's shoulders, and pulled her toward him.

"Yervant is right. We have to keep our spirits up. We're from here, we're from there. We are complicated. Why should we choose?"

Joseph had always been afraid of losing himself, but never dared to admit it. He was looking for a compass to show him the way. Like a traveler in a fragile skiff, buffeted by high waves and the endless ocean, he was looking for a way to steady himself. In the storm, his cello had given him the shelter he sought, a closed space far from the world and its dangers, far from his tumultuous family. Yet that evening, in the little Brooklyn theater, Yervant had held out a helping hand. Joseph could now leave the protected world he had constructed, reconcile himself with the past and envisage the future. From now on, cello in hand, he was strong enough to face the light of day.

Figaro jumped on Joseph's knees. He stroked the cat's head. "OK, we've chatted enough for today," he said. "It's time to go to bed."

Joseph had a fitful sleep, dreaming about a craggy Alpine path. He was walking behind his father, who was moving quickly. From time to time, Eric Landolt turned toward his son without a word, and gave him a sign of encouragement, but it wasn't needed. Joseph had grown and he could now keep up with his father. Swift and firm-footed. They were alone in a rare moment of intimacy against this beautiful backdrop. The July light threw radiant beams on the mountain tops, and the heads of the blue gentians stood out boldly amidst the beds of rhododendrons. They seemed to be seeking some protection, some guardian angel. Further on, the transparent waters of a stream hurtled down the slope. They sometimes passed people walking in the opposite direction, and would no doubt reach the nearest village in the afternoon. They exchanged short greetings, but at this altitude, words were few; it was important to remain silent and preserve your strength.

Joseph and Eric climbed up a smooth rock. Now they were sitting on a sloping ledge. Eric took some bread out of his backpack, which had left marks of perspiration on his shoulders. He split the rolls open with his penknife, filling them with slices of hard-boild egg and ham. He held the food out to his son. Joseph was really thirsty, and drank straight from the bottle. Once they had finished eating, Eric pushed himself to the edge of the rock, hanging his legs in the air, and invited Joseph to join him. Joseph hesitated, feeling dizzy. "Come on, I've got you," his father said, reassuringly. "Lean on me. You'll be fine." Joseph inched forward. On the other side of the valley, the snowy peaks of the Swiss Alps were covered with snow. The boy closed his eyes, but then he stated, with absolute certainty, "See those mountains down there? We're in Armenia." Eric, who didn't understand this twist on geography, corrected him. "You think you're in Caucasia? You should be so lucky! Those are the Dents du Midi. Don't you recognize them?" Joseph began to laugh. "Oh yes? Are you sure? Get another map and look carefully." He gave his father the binoculars and added, "You'll see that the scenery has changed." To Eric's surprise, the binoculars turned into a kaleidoscope, mixing the landscape and the colors. The peaks became superimposed on top of one another, the valleys shrank, the paths disappeared. And the world did an about-face.

High in the sky, a sparrow hawk flew away, swooped round, and then came back toward them.

XII

Taxi

Every year, at the end of September, the International Committee of the Red Cross organized a cultural evening in its museum on the Avenue of Peace. They called it an *event* rather than a *concert,* since the anglicized term *event* gave the evening additional prestige. It began with a classical music concert and ended with a cocktail hour where premium liquor was served, along with jumbo shrimp and canapés of (imitation) caviar. It was a perfect moment, one of the high points of the season. Profits went to humanitarian initiatives such as the eradication of malaria or the construction of artesian wells. The local élite (that is to say, Protestant high society) attended the evening's festivities, which were covered by several TV channels the following day. Their enthusiasm was born of good conscience. Had they skipped the event, taken it too lightly or not stayed long enough, it would have been taken the wrong way. Above all, it was important to respect tradition. Although they were at home, so to speak (everyone knew each other and recognized each other in this small town), the audience scrupulously mixed familiarity, hugs, virile handshakes, and small talk. They would ask "How is your mother?" or, lowering their tone, "I heard that Florence was sick…" and, eventually, "Bye, we'll be in touch!" Money flowed freely but discreetly: nothing was more vulgar than ostentation. In this sense, any allusion to affluence would have reflected a grave lack of taste. It was absolutely forbidden to make reference, however oblique, to material possessions. For example, you would never think of mentioning a German sports car or a fancy ski resort, even if, of course, you possessed the former or went to the latter.

The most subtle part of these niceties consisted of deciding how to address people, thus speaking informally or formally, depending on whom you were talking to. It was important to choose wisely, since the rigid class stratification demanded the appropriate linguistic code. Any mistake would leave the guilty vulnerable to retaliation, either to condemnation or banishment from this society.

That autumn, the organization of the evening had been entrusted to Inés Miranda, whose Guatemalan origins might have put certain participants off were she not married to a well-established local lawyer, Horace Reverdin Lacour. As the date drew near, Inés decided that this year's event should consist of a gala. Rummaging greedily through the shelves of a chic boutique, and ignoring the tentative advice of an intimidated sales person, she set her heart on a frilly dress, which would doubtless look too *pink* for the Calvinist surroundings. She did not care. She wanted that dress, and she was going to have it. Delighted with her selection, she was just emerging from the dressing room when her phone rang. And she received the news. The concert soloist, a Chinese cellist, had just had an accident. The taxi transporting him had swerved unexpectedly, colliding with a truck coming the other way. The musician was seriously injured. He had hurt his hand and suffered a concussion, and had been taken by ambulance to a local hospital. Several x-rays confirmed the emergency examination. It would be several months until the patient could play his cello again. Inés Miranda was not the kind of person to be deterred by this turn of events. However, when she heard the diagnosis, which was confirmed by a second medical opinion, she did suffer a moment of unsteadiness. How could she find another artist on such short notice? Who could possibly replace such a highly regarded, well-renowned soloist? Indeed, how could she avoid a fiasco? Inés called an agency that specialized in event planning. She was greeted cordially by the manager, who promised to comb through his vast network of musicians and find an alternative. But the research turned up no possibilities. No artist was available on that date, except an Australian, impossible to reach because he was trekking in the Himalayas. Her evening event abandoned to fate, Inés examined her options and was suddenly hit by a flash of inspiration. She thought about Joseph Landolt, the grandson of Aram Simonian, with whom she had shared a romantic relationship for several years. In particular, she remembered Joseph's emotional rendition of *The Swan* at Aram's funeral.

"You want to hire a student for the Red Cross concert?" Horace Reverdin Lacour was skeptical when he learned of his wife's plans.

"What other choice do I have?" Inés inquired, circling across the room, while Horace, ensconced in his Empire chair, opened a box of cigars.

"It's a senseless risk! Some people pay a fortune to go to this event, and they're very demanding. You know them!"

"You may be right, but I'm going to… uh, how do you say it…?" Inés wondered aloud, "butter them up. I'll introduce this young man as the star of tomorrow, like this: 'In a preview showing, we present *the* discovery of the year!'"

"To summarize: a little snobbery, a little pedagogy, and you come out on top? Are you taking them for idiots?"

"Not at all," Inés replied, a smile on her lips. "And plus, Joseph isn't a student now. I met his mother in town, and she told me that he had graduated. She struts around as proud as a peacock!"

"OK, OK," Horace muttered, lighting up a Cuban cigar. Do whatever you feel like. You're in charge."

"Thanks, baby. That's exactly what I wanted to hear. I'm going to call the boy as soon as possible and tell him the good news. Ah! Another thing. I've found a really pretty dress for the evening. Would you like to see it?"

"I'd just like to know how much it cost!"

"Listen, I've had enough trouble today, so don't give me even more. I forget how much this little number went for," Inés said, as if she had conveniently forgotten. "Wait a minute." She came back a few minutes later in her new outfit, the flounces suiting her sixty-year-old figure.

"Very nice choice," said Horace, admiringly. "But the color…"

"What do you mean, the color?"

"Your dress is, well, really pink."

"Horace, I know you're a great lawyer, but you would never make it in the world of fashion!"

Inés went back to her room, and examined herself from head to toe in a full-length mirror. She was reassured. The dress was truly becoming, except for one fold of fabric that needed readjusting at the waist. "Too bad for everyone who prefers black," she thought. "It's not a funeral!" Relishing the comments that were sure to be whispered from person to person on the evening of the concert, she picked up the phone and called Joseph. She had hardly said a word when he recognized her inimitable accent.

"Joseph! You remember me!"

"Yes, of course! How could I possibly forget you?"

"We old ladies from Guatemala have no need to introduce ourselves," Inés said, bursting into the loud laughter that had once seduced Aram. "We're betrayed by our accent! How are you, my dear Joseph?"

He told her about his year in New York, and Inés let him speak without interrupting. He spoke of the exams he had passed, the praise the jury had given him, and imitated the voice of his teacher, Elmar Bruder, who, faithful to habit, didn't hesitate to take the credit. "I was the one to notice this boy at his first audition, and I pushed him," he had said. "I made him work his behind off whenever he faced a problem.

I often lost it with him, but in the end, *we* managed."

"Magnificent," Inés said. "And now your career is about to begin."

"Not overnight. I have to make myself known, build up my contacts. That takes time."

"No, no, immediately."

"You're dreaming, Inés."

"Absolutely not. I've found you your first assignment."

Joseph murmured something in disbelief, but had no time to ask questions.

"It's very easy. Tomorrow, you get on a plane, and three days later, you are playing whatever piece you like at a Red Cross concert."

"Uh… can you explain all that to me, please?"

She described the situation in a few words: the importance of the event, the swerving of the taxi, the injuries of the cellist.

"It's impossible to replace the poor cellist. You can imagine the panic, and we've looked for a substitute everywhere. So I'm counting on you," Inés proclaimed in a definitive tone.

"I'm very honored that you thought of me, but it's impossible!"

"Why, pray tell?"

"I'm not good enough, that's all," Joseph replied. He was aware of the prominence of the musician in question, and had no difficulty imagining how disappointed the audience would be when discovering that the eminent soloist had been replaced by an unknown cellist recently graduated from a conservatory, no matter how reputable it may be. "These charity evenings are very demanding," he added, "and I'll be the joke of the night for your banker friends and their charming wives. Anyway, what does Horace think?"

Inés was about to embellish the truth to further her argument. But she stopped herself.

"You want to know everything? Unfortunately, Horace agrees with you. But that doesn't mean that he's right. And neither are you!"

The line fell silent. Then, suddenly, Inés dug up the winning argument.

"Joseph, you'll be thinking about your grandfather as you play. Imagine the pleasure he would have had when he heard you…"

Sitting in his Brooklyn apartment, Joseph thought back to Aram's coffin, at the funeral where he had played the cello for his grandfather. He remembered coming out of the church, where Inés, dressed in a coat with a fur collar, approached his family. Nobody knew her, except for him. To their surprise and anger, he had shown his mother and his uncle the extensive correspondence between the lady from Guatemala and his grandfather from Armenia.

"OK, Inés, you win," Joseph said. "But if this turns out badly, promise me you'll ask the Red Cross to send an ambulance!"

Figaro looked at Joseph inquisitively. He had been paying close attention to the conversation.

Joseph was on the plane to Geneva. He was uncomfortable in the narrow seat, and tried to stretch out his long legs, but there was no room. He couldn't manage to sleep. He took out a notebook to jot down his thoughts, attempting to recapture the strong impression that Yervant Manoukian's play had made on him.

This actor in the orange sweater says important things. He sings them, mimes them, lives them.

'About-Face,' I love that title and the movement. (Joseph underlines 'movement.') *You come, you go, you leave, you*

204

come back. First, tragedy – poverty, exile, the mother, the crying – then the trip, then the playacting. OK, I agree, it's dark, but at the end, surprise and laughter carry it through. It's not a rigid world we live in. Sadness can get torn away, just as you tear off clothes when they become too small for you. We defy sadness, or rather melancholy. We defy our sweet and our insidious feelings. We're willing victims of a temptation so strong we can't resist it, like a kid who is offered chocolate fondant. In the end, who is this Yervant? A man who has overcome his inhibitions? The sensitive type, cashing in on his vitality? Or a poet who is simply making up a story? It doesn't matter. It doesn't even matter if his story is true or not. The energy that he was transmitting hit me straight in the face. Like a powerful gift. He doesn't know this (obviously), but it was him who got me and Greta to make up. That was lucky, because things were souring between us… Above all, he reconciled me with myself. I finally understood. I don't have to choose between different places, between the past and the present. I shouldn't separate them. Instead, I should connect them. Add, never subtract. Avoid the containment. Containment, what a terrible word - it's like isolation, confinement. We were thrown out of our land, with no mercy or hope to return. But that's too bad, because today, we own the world. The sky's the limit.

The cabin had fallen into darkness. Joseph put down his pen and dozed off. He dreamed that he was no longer on a plane, but was playing the Fauré sonata without the score. Halfway through the second movement, he drew a blank and needed to stop. It was pretty disconcerting. Elmar Bruder was in the first row. He leaned over to Greta and whispered in her ear. Then there was jeering by a Chinese cellist and an Australian alpinist. Joseph was humiliated. He got up, put the instrument on the seat and ran out of the room.

He woke up as the wheels hit the tarmac.

The night before the concert, Inés gave Joseph some instructions.

"We're going to take the audience by surprise. We're going to blow them away…"

"I don't understand," Joseph replied. He knew that Inés had a lively imagination, and he was a little uneasy.

"No, it's simple. Take a step back and think. The audience is expecting to see a famous musician walk onto the stage in a tuxedo, no smile on his face, certain that he has already won them over. That's magnificent of course, but it's kind of boring because it is the typical soirée, so predictable. You'll be different. You'll show up in jeans and a blue jacket. I'll be there to introduce you: the young musician with a bright future ahead of him. You see?"

"All I foresee is catastrophe. I've been dragged into a film noir."

"No pessimism at your age, my dearest! Just tell yourself that you'll be a success. Think about the Olympic Games."

"Oh yes? Why?"

"That's the name of the game. Why? Well, I don't really know. Faster, higher, stronger… That sounds vague, but try to visualize what I'm saying."

"Um, yeah … But sometimes athletes miss their mark though," Joseph said, scowling before he added, "Now, I'll leave you, Mrs. Organizer of Good Works. I have to go and practice the sonata with the pianist. See you soon."

The next evening, the residents of old Geneva arrived en masse at the Red Cross Museum. A procession of high society ambassadors streamed through, the ladies on the arms of greying gentlemen. When they had all sat and stopped talking, Inés appeared triumphantly on the stage, dressed in her pink attire and with a microphone in her hand.

She reeled off some welcoming remarks and, exaggerating her Spanish accent in the odd hope of making herself understood better that way, appealed to the generosity of the audience, defending the cause of exiled peoples in Europe. Neither her tone nor her appearance went unnoticed. Some eyebrows were raised in irritation. Surprised whispers ran up and down the rows, and one affluent but indiscreet donor took a cellphone out of his pocket in an expression of disapproval. The glare of the screen stood out as a blemish on the darkened room. Inés had been expecting these reactions, and took pleasure in observing them. "We can nudge them a little, both their attitudes and their wallets…" she thought, sending an imperceptible signal to Horace Reverdin Lacour. Dressed in a classic suit, he did not know whether to admire his wife's brilliance or deplore her brazen behavior. Then Inés changed her tone. Lowering her voice, she solemnly described the accident that had befallen the Chinese cellist in the taxi and the injuries he had sustained. "However," she continued, "this tragedy has given his replacement the unique opportunity to showcase his talent." And she added: "This evening, Ladies and Gentlemen, I have the great pleasure of introducing Joseph Simonian, who has come from New York to play to us Gabriel Fauré's Cello Sonata No. 1 in D minor, Opus 109."

When Joseph and the pianist went onto the stage, a feeling of sympathy radiated out from the crowd. Nobody was bothered by their uncombed hair or their badly-polished shoes. The cellist sat to the right of the Steinway, and tuned the cello with the aid of the piano. Then the lights went down and the concert began. The energy and sensitivity of the interpretation immediately won the audience's hearts. Among the spectators were Anne and Eric Landolt, sitting in the next to last row, holding their breath as their son played. When Fauré's final chords faded away and the artists bowed to enthusiastic applause, the proud parents took each other by the hand, gazing at Joseph in his moment of triumph. Their little son, who used to hide behind the curtains, had become an adult.

The sonata gave way to champagne and hors d'oeuvres. Throngs of people, each more elegant than the next, inundated the musicians with congratulations. A man with a falsetto voice came up to Joseph and gave him his card, saying, "I'm Samuel Randall. Call me tomorrow." He was a promoter, well known in classical music circles, whose network stretched all over the world. Once Samuel Randall had shuffled off toward the buffet, the banker who had inconsiderately taken out his cellphone stepped up to speak to the heroes of the evening. He exchanged some niceties and criticized the acoustics in the room, but then off-handedly offered to lend Joseph a Venetian-crafted eighteenth-century cello. "We've had this instrument in my family for a long time," the banker told him, "but nobody knows how to play it. You may as well take advantage of it." That evening, in the Red Cross Museum, under the benevolent eye of Gabriel Fauré, Joseph's future made an about-face.

Her face as pink as her dress, Inés fluttered from guest to guest, stopping to talk to some and waving at others. From time to time, caught up in a wave of satisfaction, she would accept a petit four from one of the waiters. When she found Joseph, she leaned over to him and whispered,

"So, my dear, are you happy? You played really well. You won them all over, these donors. Thanks to you, we'll make a pretty penny! Thank you, my Armenian!"

"Inés, you made a mistake when you told them my name."

"Oh yes?" asked Inés innocently. "What did I say?"

"My name is Landolt," Joseph reminded her.

"Oh, and I said Simonian, right? I'm so absent-minded. It's my age, what do you expect?"

Inés squinted and gave Joseph a passing kiss that left a mark on his pale cheek.

When the last lights were turned off and the museum fell silent, Joseph suggested to the pianist that they have a drink (then two, then three…) in a nearby bar. They were relieved to have completed the task that they had been given so unexpectedly, and talked late into the night. Time stood still, leaving them full of enthusiasm and hope. Barriers and obstacles had disappeared. Saying "tomorrow," and "next year," they talked of music, love, and music again. Looking ahead to the future, they saw countless possibilities, endless opportunities.

They said goodbye at dawn, and a light breeze drifted over the city. Joseph called a taxi and gave the driver the address of the house on the lake. As the car navigated the sleepy streets and crossed Mont Blanc Bridge to the other side of Lake Geneva, the steady noise of the engine rocked Joseph to sleep. Half an hour later, he opened his eyes in surprise. It took him a few seconds to figure out where he was. He paid the fare, rounding it up with a generous tip. The driver was surprised, thanking him several times before letting him out. As the taxi drove off, Joseph was hit with a shock. He was missing something. His heart beating, he realized that he had forgotten his cello in the trunk, the one he had had since he was an adolescent. He waved his arms frantically, hoping to attract the driver's attention, but it was too late. The taxi had already turned the corner. For a while, you could still hear the sound of the engine, but it gradually faded away to silence.

Harry Koumrouyan

Epilogue

The Red Cross Museum concert raised a substantial sum of money for charitable works. People's generosity that evening no doubt gave them a direct passport to paradise, while also giving Joseph Landolt the unexpected chance to launch his musical career. Assistance soon came his way via the promoter he had met after the gala, the one whose professional network stretched far and wide. This led to a series of opportunities, in smaller towns and then in large concert halls, thanks to the enthusiastic reception of critics: "Young cellist with remarkable talent blends sensitivity with technical excellence…" etc. Joseph took with him the Venetian cello that the banker had made available for his use. He treated it with utmost care, like a jewel, and often drew amused or rude remarks from those around him. (Recently, while flying, he had needed to leave his seat for a moment, and asked the young woman next to him to watch the instrument carefully. She burst out laughing. "Are you afraid it will fly away? It's your baby, right?" He was careful not to reply, because he did not want to let on how tremendously valuable the cello was.)

All that traveling was not without its difficulties. He was often lonely, and thought about Greta, who had stayed in Brooklyn. He was anxious to see her again. That evening, in the far-off town where he had been on a concert tour, he couldn't sleep. He lit his bedside lamp and picked up his notebook.

Airport. Hotel. Practice. Concert. Bad night's sleep. Another move. Hotel (different, but similar). Same menu. Same television channel with world news ad infinitum. Same stage fright, same apprehensiveness. And what if they don't like me anymore? I can just see the headline: "Joseph Landolt gave a disappointing performance. He rose too far, too fast... All upcoming concerts are canceled. He is not a prodigy after all, but an imposter." Before my concerts, I picked up a chestnut in our garden on the lake and put it into my pocket. I don't tell anyone I need a good luck charm, or they'll think I'm some kind of rookie. I have a migraine tonight. I shouldn't complain. I know how lucky I am and I know of musicians who would kill both parents to be in my place. But I can talk freely to this notebook and explain the nerves I have when I'm in the wings just before a concert. I want to throw up, or run away... Sometimes my cello is my enemy. It is a demanding ruler, two and a half centuries old, but it has kept its velvet voice intact. It wants to break out of the case. It loves being on stage, ready to conquer the audience and drink in their applause. So we meet again, my cello and I, as if we were making love after a long separation.

Greta just called me on the phone and told me she'd like to introduce me to her parents. We're going to Armenia in two months. I'll be playing at a conservatory in Yerevan. That's a strange feeling. Is Armenia my home? Or not? Or just a little? Well, we'll see. I've never been there, and I've never really been interested in going. Perhaps vaguely curious, but that's it. Greta is going to show me the country. She's going to explain where she comes from and I'll understand her better that way (and perhaps myself, too). A week after we get there, my parents will come and join us. Those two will never give up fighting, making up, and fighting again. That's just what they do. It's a fitful love affair. I know, it's strange, but I've learned to accept it. I just accept them as they are. (As if I had any choice!)

Arthur will come with them. He's definitely going to tell us about his new girlfriend. My uncle just can't sit still. He has one love affair after the other. I wish Aram and my grandmother were still here. We would have had a family gathering in the garden. I can just see it now. Everyone would raise their glass in turn and say something. I can hear Aram's booming voice: "Pasha, I'm drinking to your success and happiness." Then, I'm sure that he would turn to Greta and say, "We're so happy to have you here with us. Take good care of Joseph. He's my only grandson, you know." Before saying goodbye, he would lean over and with the accent that he always kept, whisper, "Pasha, you made a good choice. She's very pretty. Are you getting married soon?"

It was a beautiful spring in Yerevan. On Republic Square, water sprang from the fountains, falling in rainbow-colored streams, tumbling into the bowls and then onto the pink marble tiles that reflected the monuments. An old lady came up to Greta and Joseph with some bunches of lilacs hung on a cart. She held them out to Joseph and asked him to choose a bouquet. He took a few coins from his pocket and gave the flowers to Greta. The seller gave them a toothless smile and walked off, stooped over.

They got to Abovian Street. In the distance they could see the snowy peaks of Mount Ararat looking over the Armenian Plateau. It was the volcano where Noah's Ark had come to rest. They stopped at a bar. In a dark corner, some chess players were focused intensely on their game, and from time to time, one of them took a piece and placed it firmly on the edge of the table. One of the pieces, maybe the queen, fell to the floor, scaring a skinny dog who was scurrying around under the chairs. Joseph and Greta ate nuts and dates and had a coffee, prepared in the local style. Then Greta tipped the cup over onto the saucer, and slowly turned it around seven times, letting the coffee dregs run down onto the flat surface. She picked up the cup again and carefully looked at the ridges and furrows, now dry, that the coffee had traced on the china.

"Are you reading the future?" Joseph asked, amused. He knew the custom.

"Of course!" replied Greta. "So, can you see anything?"

"Yes, vaguely. A maze, lines, circles…"

"That form…"

"I don't know. Abstract art? Or an alphabet?"

"You need to use your imagination, Joseph! Look carefully."

Joseph passed his hand through his hair.

"Give me a second. I'm used to figuring out sheet music. Notes, eighths, and flats, not coffee dregs! Let me think. Oh yes, there, in the corner, I can see a tree with branches stretching up to the sky."

"OK, carry on. Behind the tree…"

"There's a bird flying off. Like yesterday."

The night before, they had gone down to Lake Sevan. There were seagulls flying in wide circles high above, and the color of the water was shifting with the fading light. They were sitting in front of a monastery built on a peninsula. Grey rivers and waterfalls cascaded into the lake, which was so wide that it seemed like an ocean, its sparkling surface disappearing over the horizon. In the sober and austere panorama of such heights, the view seemed so different from Joseph's memories of Lake Geneva. He was overcome by a feeling of tranquility and peace that made all his fears dissipate. Until then, he had had difficulty assembling the disparate pieces of the puzzle that his ancestors had left behind. He sometimes said to himself in a low voice: "I don't want to carry that torch." But that evening, on the banks of Lake Sevan, he found the inner homeland he had been seeking for so long. Armenia, his Armenia, was beating in his veins. It was stronger than reality, lighter than the past. From now on, the tragedy could fade away. He was going to be twenty-five years old, and a path was opening up before him, a path that belonged to him alone. He would dedicate his music to the victims of the genocide sometimes, just as you give a thought to a long-lost friend whose shadow is slowly blurring over, but one that you will never forget. Joseph knew it. When it was time, today or in a thousand years, the unburied victims would rise up from the fields and ditches where their bodies had been thrown. Like ghosts revived, they would emerge from the shadows where they had been silently waiting to disrupt their assassins' slumber. Untouched by time, they would see justice proclaimed on heaven and earth.

Little by little, darkness came over Lake Sevan. A half-moon appeared through the clouds, shimmering in the still waters. Joseph pulled Greta's warm body toward him and took her hand, and they remained like that, silent and motionless, in the Armenian night.

Harry Koumrouyan

ABOUT THE TRANSLATOR

Kim Sanabria was born in London and lives in New York City. A former university professor, she holds a BA in Modern Languages from the University of Bradford (Combined Honours in French and Spanish), an MA in TESOL (Teaching English to Speakers of Other Languages) from Hunter College, The City University of New York, and a PhD in Spanish from Columbia University. She has published numerous textbooks for English language learners.

Harry Koumrouyan

BOOKS PUBLISHED BY CREATETANK
available where books are sold!

Star Witness by Orlando Ferrand, 2018
Poetry
Bronx Rhapsody by Maria Meli, 2018
Poetry
The White Shirt Project: An Intimate Look into the Lights
and Shadows of My Life by Jose Ramon Medina, 2023
Memoir
Such a Dangerous Silence by Harry Koumrouyan,
translated from the French by Kim Sanabria, 2023
Fiction

Harry Koumrouyan

Harry Koumrouyan